STAR WARS
THE HIGH REPUBLIC

RACE to CRASHPOINT TOWER

DANIEL JOSÉ OLDER

ILLUSTRATIONS BY
PETUR ANTONSSON

For Azul

Printed in the United States of America

First Edition, June 2021

10 9 8 7 6 5 4 3 2 1

FAC-034274-21134

ISBN 978-1-368-06066-0

Library of Congress Control Number on file

Design by Soyoung Kim, Scott Piehl, and Leigh Zieske

Visit the official *Star Wars* website at: www.starwars.com

STAR WARS
THE HIGH REPUBLIC

The galaxy celebrates. With the dark days of the hyperspace disaster behind them, Chancellor Lina Soh pushes ahead with the latest of her GREAT WORKS. The Republic Fair will be her finest hour, a celebration of peace, unity, and hope on the frontier world of Valo.

But an insatiable horror appears on the horizon. One by one, planets fall as the carnivorous DRENGIR consume all life in their path. As Jedi Master AVAR KRISS leads the battle against this terror, Nihil forces gather in secret for the next stage of MARCHION RO'S diabolical plan.

Only the noble JEDI KNIGHTS stand in Ro's way, but even the protectors of light and life are not prepared for the terrible darkness that lies ahead. . . .

STAR WARS TIMELINE

THE HIGH REPUBLIC

FALL OF THE JEDI

REIGN OF THE EMPIRE

THE PHANTOM MENACE

ATTACK OF THE CLONES

THE CLONE WARS

REVENGE OF THE SITH

THE BAD BATCH

SOLO: A STAR WARS STORY

AGE OF REBELLION

THE NEW REPUBLIC

RISE OF THE FIRST ORDER

REBELS

ROGUE ONE:
A STAR WARS
STORY

A NEW HOPE

THE EMPIRE
STRIKES BACK

RETURN OF
THE JEDI

THE
MANDALORIAN

RESISTANCE

THE FORCE
AWAKENS

THE LAST JEDI

THE RISE OF
SKYWALKER

PART
ONE

CHAPTER
ONE

Sitting cross-legged on an old starfighter pilot seat, Ram Jomaram closed his eyes and tried to block out all the clatter and commotion outside. There was plenty to block out: dignitaries and visitors from across the known galaxy were converging on the scenic mountains and forests of Valo for the first Republic Fair in ages. Most of Lonisa City's residents were putting final touches on banners, cooking scrumptious food, and preparing guest quarters. Pretty soon they'd be gathered at the almost fully constructed Jedi temple to welcome the Chancellor herself to Valo.

Lonisa City, where Ram had grown up, was a small place. People knew and looked out for each other; it seemed light-years away from the ongoing grind and rumble of the rest of the galaxy. But over the past few weeks, Ram had felt the rising tide of all that sudden attention, the hubbub and fuss seeming to get louder and louder as the many eyes of the Republic turned to Valo. So much prep had gone into this gigantic event, and there was still so much to do!

But!

None of that mattered.

All that mattered was this very moment.

Ram had slyly mentioned to Master Kunpar that one of the security team's speeder bikes was out of commission with a faulty gasket hub, and all the state mechanics were busy setting up the light show; sooooo . . . Master Kunpar had grumbled and fussed with his chin tentacles some before finally relenting, but he had, and that was why Ram got to be here, in his favorite place on the planet: a dingy, dim garage full of rusty mechanical parts and tools.

The team of repair Bonbraks scurried back and forth on the shelves around him, chattering at each other and futzing with various smaller projects, but otherwise, Jedi

Padawan Ram Jomaram was in the most peaceful state he knew: all alone in the garage, a small shed in the back grotto of the Jedi living quarters.

No complicated rules or protocols to follow, no ancient wise Masters to show the correct deference to. Just metal and bolts and plastoid and some big-eared, long-tailed fur balls who made plenty of squeaky fuss but mostly minded their own business.

Ram was one with the Force, and the Force was with Ram, he reminded himself. Here, in this peaceful, grease-stained hideaway, he could give over fully to the quiet, powerful place inside. All around him, a small constellation of speeder parts hovered. There were the leather seat and metal casing over the main hub—he could swing those out of the way for the moment. Here was the engine, with its grill and gaskets and piping. Here was the fuse box that would fit in alongside the retrovaporizer and connect into the rest of the machinery. And here was the repulsorlift hub, still shiny with residue from when it had spluttered fission oil earlier, during a routine patrol.

"You must see the whole for the whole," Master Kunpar had told Ram so, so many times, "and each part for the role it plays—not for what you want it to be, not for what you fear it to be. Just for what it is."

He made it sound so easy. Also, he was probably talking about meditation techniques and combat maneuvers most of the times he said it—true Jedi stuff. But for Ram, mechanics *was* meditation. And anyway, the Force was everywhere, right? He figured his master would be pleased he was finding practical applications for all that wisdom. Hopefully!

Ram could feel the quiet thrum of each segment, the tiny vibrations in the air that described them as they floated in a slow circle around him, that faraway trill within the hub that rang just a fraction of a note dissonant from the rest of the parts. *Each part for the role it plays . . .* There! That meant something was off. He knew how all the different pieces were supposed to look, feel, sound. He'd pored over the tech specs and taken apart and put back together everything mechanical within grabbing distance since he was a youngling, so he knew when the vibrations of a part didn't hum right. The shape of it had warped, probably too much heat, but how? *Not for what you want it to be, not for what you fear it to be . . .* Something else must be wrong.

He knew most Jedi didn't use the Force this way, but what fun was it having cool abilities if you didn't investigate the inner workings of busted old mechanical parts with them, right? That was how Ram saw it, anyway. He loved gears and wires and the secrets they seemed to hold, and he loved feeling the Force flow through him, connecting him to the larger universe. Combining the two was just about the best thing ever.

Ram continued his scan, his mind sliding along the accelerator foot pedals, steering mechanism, control panels, and exhaust pipe. *Just for what it is.* He had caught the faintest sense of something, a teensy, off-key ding, when—

"GREETINGS, MASTER RAM!" the metallic voice of V-18 called from the doorway.

"I must see the whole for the whole," Ram whispered, eyes still closed. The speeder parts faltered in their slow rotation, dipped toward the ground. "And each part for the role it plays."

"*JomaramaRam do chunda mota mota-ta!*" an irritated Bonbrak countered. That was probably Tip, the youngest and surliest of the crew. Several others concurred loudly.

"Well, there's no need to be rude," V-18 said.

The speeder parts slid lower. "Not for what I want it to be, not for what I fear it to be," Ram growled. "Just for what it is."

"*Bacha no bacha kribkrib patrak!*"

"*Pratrak patrak!*"

"*JomaramaRam!*"

"I simply expressed my salutations," V-18 insisted. "I happen to be both excited to see the young Padawan and on an errand of some urgency, which is why I modulated my voice into a higher frequency and volume, for your info—"

One of the Bonbraks grunted out a squeak (almost definitely Fezmix—he was always the rowdy one), and then a metallic ding rang out and V-18 yelped.

"Unnecessary!" cried the droid.

"I MUST SEE THE WHOLE FOR THE WHOLE!" Ram hollered as all the speeder parts clattered to the floor. A single gear kept rolling in an irritating, wobbly circle after everything else had settled. He looked up to see seven pairs of beady black eyes and one glowing electronic one staring back at him.

"Oh, dear," muttered V-18.

Ram sighed, and the rolling gear finally fell over with a clank.

The Bonbraks immediately began bickering among themselves, and Ram lowered himself from the pilot seat and rubbed his eyes. "What is it, Vee-Eighteen?"

The droid had been around for the Force knew how many years, and it showed. He towered over everyone like a ridiculous rusty crate with stumpy legs. Ram had painted V-18 bright purple because people kept loading him onto ships when he was in sleep mode, thinking he was cargo. A single off-center eye glared out of each side of the boxy droid. Sometimes they blinked, which either indicated impatience or a programming glitch—Ram was never sure. "Masters Kunpar and Lege are preparing for the big event at the temple," V-18 announced. "Which is . . . quite soon, of course!"

"Okay?"

"And Masters Devo and Shonnatrucks are greeting some of the new security forces the Republic has sent for the fair before they head over for the ceremony, which is imminent."

"Vee-Eighteen . . ."

"And all the other Padawans are with them."

"Vee-Eighteen, why are you telling me the location of all the Valon Jedi?"

"Because Crashpoint Tower is glitchy."

The comms tower was outside Lonisa City proper, deep in the Farodin Woods on a hill some of the local daredevils had dubbed Crashpoint Peak. And it would be dark soon. "Well, I better take a look at it."

"No!"

Ram blinked at V-18. "Why not?"

"Because there's a matter that requires your attention more urgently," the droid said.

"Are you going to make me take you apart to access your databanks for it, or are you just going to tell me what it is?"

"My, my! There's no need to—"

"Vee-Eighteen!"

"There was an alert tripped on the security perimeter of the comms tower."

Ram's eyes went wide. A perimeter breach wasn't necessarily a big deal—probably just some forest critter. But with the Nihil attacks in the Outer Rim and the fair coming up, everyone was on high alert, so the Jedi had been instructed to treat any possible security issue as top priority. "What? Did you alert the Masters?"

V-18 shook his big boxy body and blinked irritably—this time Ram was positive that flicker was on purpose. "I just told you! The comms are glitchy! Sheesh, man!"

"So there's a security breach at the comms tower, and the comms are glitchy? And . . . Why didn't you tell me that in the first place?"

"Well, I didn't want anyone to get hurt."

Ram didn't have time to get into all the ways that didn't make sense. "We have to get out there! When was the breach?"

"One hour ago!" V-18 announced triumphantly.

"We have to go now! We gotta—" He spun around, ready to jump on the security speeder bike, and then remembered that it was in pieces all over the garage floor. And he wasn't cleared to use any of the larger transports. And walking would take too long—they'd never make it before dark, and whatever had breached the perimeter and possibly damaged the comms tower would be long gone. Which might be a good thing, because then Ram wouldn't have to confront and maybe fight it. Ram hated fighting. Well—he'd never done it, but he hated the *idea* of it. It felt like his body refused to cooperate any time even a practice battle was called for. Lightsaber training and Jedi combat maneuvers were his two worst areas, and the very thought of going face to face with an enemy made him jittery.

But it didn't matter. He was a Jedi Padawan, and he was apparently the only one around to deal with this. It was his duty, even if he would've rather spent the rest of the night tinkering. That meant he had to get out there as fast as possible.

He eyed V-18.

"First I had to go see where the Jedi Masters were, according to protocol," the droid rambled, "but the living quarters and temple were both empty! And then I tried to raise them on the comms, but . . . Why are you looking at me like that?"

An idea formulated inside Ram's mind, and once that happened, it was hard to think of anything else. He was probably squinting creepily at the droid; he was definitely assessing where different parts could fit on that bulky frame. "Do those legs retract?" Ram glanced at a spare thruster unit he'd nabbed off an old single-pilot crop sifter headed for the junk pile. Seven pairs of tiny eyes followed his gaze.

"I'll have you know that this nimble but robust physique is capable of an unpredictable number of—"

"Do they retract?" Ram shot a meaningful glance at the Bonbraks, who'd already started moving into position around V-18. He was glad they'd learned to recognize his about-to-spring-into-action face.

"Of course! No need to interr—"

"How would you feel about a mobility upgrade?"

"Well, I hardly see how you could upgrade this unparalleled appara—"

"Vee-Eighteen!"

"Why, yes, actually, I would like that quite a bit," the droid admitted.

"Let's do it!" Ram yelled, and with high-pitched squeals, the Bonbraks pounced.

"What's going on?" V-18 wailed. "Unhand me, you tiny vagrants! You're getting greasy little fingerprints on my delicate firmament!"

"This won't take long," Ram assured him.

It didn't. V-18 got enthusiastic once he realized how awesome the upgrade was going to be, and he even tried to help out some. With the Bonbraks running point on the wiring and fuses, Ram secured the propulsors to V-18 and rigged up a handy saddle with foot pedals to control acceleration. There wasn't time to add brakes, but who needed brakes, right? Okay—he did eventually, but he'd work that out later. For now, decelerating would have to do.

He shot a wistful glance at the scattered remains of the speeder, then used a foot pedal to heave himself onto V-18, who was tilted forward and hovering slightly over the ground. The seat they'd attached was pretty comfy, and the handlebars were at just the right height. Ram revved the engine once and then whooshed out the door to the cheers of the Bonbraks.

"This is actually quite enjoyable!" V-18 yelled over the whistling wind as they zoomed past the shacks on the outskirts of Lonisa City and into the Farodin Woods.

"I thought you might like it," Ram said. "The question is, can we go any faster?"

"I'm not sure that's—"

Ram pushed the accelerator pedal all the way down, and V-18 lurched into overdrive, flashing around the towering acthorn trees, then zipping up a hill and over a rocky embankment. "Woooooooooooooohooooooooo!" Ram yelled.

The sun was just starting to dip into the clouds over the distant mountain range as they burst out of the woods above the field where the comms tower was.

Ram lifted his foot off the accelerator. Something moved in the clearing ahead: a figure, standing up from where it had been crouching, then raising a long cylinder. Ram's eyes went wide. He pulled hard on the throttle and gunned the thrusters just as the first round of blaster fire smashed through the trees behind him.

"Yeeeeeeeeeee!" V-18 screeched. Another fiery shot tore over their heads. "What do we do now?"

Ram guided them behind a pile of boulders and eased into a hover. The shooting had stopped, but he could hear the angry growls of speeder engines. Way up past the branches and leaves, a few tiny lights blinked against the darkening sky. "They're going to make a run for it," Ram whispered. "Back to whatever ship brought them here." If they were more interested in getting away than finishing off Ram, that meant whatever they were up to was very important indeed. Which meant—

"I hope you're not planning to—" V-18 warned just as Ram revved up the engine.

"We gotta stop them!"

The galaxy spun around Lula Talisola in a wild, ever-flowing array of lights and colors. It was so beautiful, and it seemed to move with her; she was part of it, and it was part of her.

"Lula?"

Who would bother her at a time like this? With all these flowing stars and galaxies—

Something nudged her shoulder. "Lula!" Zeen's voice.

"Mrrgg?"

"We're almost there," Zeen said.

Where were they almost?

Trymant IV!

Lula sat up, blinking. She was on her bed in the Padawan bunk of the *Star Hopper*. She wore her silky head wrap, and around her the musty familiar smell of sleep mixed with the body odor of various beings.

Trymant IV was Zeen's homeworld. That's where they almost were. And this would be their first time back since the wreckage of a starship had burst out of hyperspace months earlier and nearly destroyed the entire planet. Zeen had saved Lula and all her friends' lives that day—and she'd done so by using the Force, even though she was just a regular citizen, not a Jedi Padawan like Lula. Zeen had been raised not to trust the Jedi, in fact, and had hidden her Force sensitivity from everyone, right up until a flaming chunk of debris had nearly crushed Lula and her friends Farzala and Qort. They'd been so distracted facing off against the Nihil—a group of masked raiders terrorizing their planet—they hadn't seen it coming, but Zeen had. She'd stopped the flaming debris in midair, saving all their lives, and nothing had been the same since. Lula had never seen someone untrained in the Force use it so naturally.

The two girls had become inseparable almost immediately, and to Lula's relief, Zeen decided to stick around with the Padawans, even though she was too old to be trained as one herself.

"You all right?" Zeen asked.

Lula rubbed that deep galactic sleep from her eyes and stretched. The hyperspace routes were still a little dicey following the Great Disaster, so they'd had to dip in and out of them, which made the journey extra long. "I'm good," she said, and then took in the worried look on her friend's magenta face, the way Zeen's Mikkian head tendrils squeezed tightly together and rippled with tiny waves. "But you're not."

Zeen looked away. "No, I'm fine."

"And I'm a horn-toed morglesnap." Lula rolled her eyes and patted the bed. "Sit."

Zeen did as she was told, still not meeting Lula's gaze.

Of course Zeen was upset. She was about to be home again, and she was returning with the very people her friends and family distrusted the most: the Jedi. Word had probably gotten out that she'd used the Force—it wasn't the kind of thing people just forgot about. Worse, Zeen's childhood friend Krix Kamarat had seen it all happen. She'd saved him, too, but the ungrateful twerp seemed to hate her for it, and he'd run off with the Nihil raiders.

"Okay, I'm not fine," Zeen admitted. "But I will be." She managed a sad smile.

Lula picked up a pillow and whapped Zeen in the face with it. "Not good enough!"

"Wow! Unhelpful!" Zeen yelled, shoving Lula right off the bed.

"Padawan Talisola and Zeen Mrala!" The robotic voice of PZ1-3 boomed over the ship's comm. "We are approaching Trymant IV! Report to the deck immediately!"

Zeen and Lula traded glances. "You got this," Lula said. "And we'll be by your side no matter what."

Zeen nodded, and Lula could tell she was doing her best to hold it together.

❀

Jedi Master Kantam Sy paced back and forth on the deck of the *Star Hopper* as PZ1-3 navigated them closer and closer to Trymant IV. Sy was tall and slender, with sharp cheekbones and an impressive topknot. They seemed older than their actual age, in part because they often walked startlingly slow as a form of meditation. But Lula had seen Master Sy in action, and that gentle easygoing demeanor was nowhere to be seen when lives were on the line.

Lula and Zeen slid into the seats at their stations. It was strange to be the only two young people on the *Hopper*. The bridge was normally alive with chattering and laughter, Farzala cracking jokes and Qort explaining something complicated while the others gossiped or traded tips. But everyone else was off fighting an army of carnivorous plant creatures called the Drengir, and only Zeen and Lula were left.

Stars shimmered in the darkness outside the transparent dome covering the whole top level of the *Hopper*. Lula and her friends would sometimes take their sleeping bags up and lie on their backs late at night, watching the galaxy spin past.

"Listen up, listen up," Master Sy said, already in action mode. "We'll be landing in a moment. The last time we were here, things were very different, of course. We had some confrontations—"

"Almost died a whole bunch," Lula added helpfully.

"And made a new friend!" Sy said, flashing a winning smile at Zeen. "Now we're here for a very specific reason, and that's to follow up on a lead from Jedi Vernestra Rwoh. I'll let her fill you in."

The small blue image of a girl not much older than Lula flickered up from the holo. This was Vernestra Rwoh? She had a slender, kind face and long straight hair. She wore the traditional temple robes, both simple and ornate, and stood with her back very straight. But how could she be so young? A prickly flash of emotion rose within Lula, and she tried to push it away. Envy. A very un-Jedi-like feeling indeed. She crinkled her nose with the strain of getting her emotions under control.

Ever since she could remember, Lula Talisola had been determined to be the greatest Jedi of all time. She knew this ambition wasn't very Jedi-like, either, but she figured she had time to get that part under control amid all her other training. And anyway, if she trained hard enough and excelled at every possible skill, she wouldn't have to worry about becoming the best; she just *would* be the best!

So she studied and trained and meditated, at least twice as much as all the other Padawans she knew. And she stayed at the top of her clan. She figured she was on track, for the most part. Meeting Zeen, seeing what she could do with the Force, even without training—that had thrown Lula at first, sure. But Zeen had quickly become one of her best friends, and Lula found she couldn't be bothered to wonder how amazing a Jedi Zeen would've been if she had been raised in the Jedi Order instead of suppressing her Force sensitivity—not when they were having so much fun together.

But Vernestra had already become a full Knight and she was so young! Who was this girl?

A sharp nudge from Zeen ripped Lula from her spiral of overthinking.

"Ow! What?" she whispered.

"You're doing it again," Zeen hissed back.

"Doing what?"

"Thinking too hard about something and not paying attention to what's going on around you!"

Lula was extra annoyed because her friend was right. "How do you know?"

"You're grinding your teeth."

"And so," Vernestra was explaining, "I looked deeper

into the files from the Trymant IV disaster and discovered the story of your cohort and Zeen Mrala." She nodded at Zeen, who acknowledged her with a shy wave. "The Nihil raiders you came into contact with might have something to do with the ones I faced on Wevo. From what I understand, their attack on Trymant IV didn't follow their usual raid patterns."

An awkward moment passed; the young Jedi looked directly at Zeen. She was waiting for Zeen to say something, Lula realized. But Zeen's head tendrils pointed directly down, tensed, and her brow was furrowed. The whole mess with Krix and everything that had happened since was too much to get into, especially with a strange Jedi on a flickering hologram.

"Is it, ah, true," Vernestra said, her voice suddenly gentle and uncertain, "that one of your closest friends ran off with the masked raiders?"

Zeen nodded once, her whole face a frown.

"We believe that the elder the Nihil rescued from the Emergence on Trymant IV—"

"Elder Tromak," Zeen said.

"Yes." Vernestra looked solemn. "We think he may have had some ancient information that the Nihil were after. . . . Master Yoda went to investigate—we think—"

"Still no word from him?" Lula asked, trying not to sound too worried. Lula thought Master Yoda was the greatest Jedi the galaxy had known, and he'd been with her and the other Padawans for most of their adventures on the *Star Hopper*. Nothing had felt the same without him around, but she always figured he'd come back.

"Nothing," Vernestra said. "But in the meantime we must keep investigating." She turned to Master Sy and nodded respectfully. "We were hoping you and your Padawans could investigate for us, Master Sy. And with Zeen's help, maybe you could get some answers from the elders who weren't taken by the Nihil."

"We'll do our best," Master Sy said. "Right, Zeen?"

"Yes, Master Sy."

"I'm sure you already know," Vernestra said, "that these raiders are ruthless, unpredictable, and extremely dangerous. We don't think any are still in the Trymant system, but that doesn't mean they won't come back."

"We do know," Master Sy said, with perhaps an edge of pride in their voice. "My Padawans have already faced them down several times."

"Entering Trymant system," PZ1-3 announced from the pilot seat.

Vernestra nodded at Sy, then turned to Lula and Zeen. "May the Force be with you all." And she was gone.

"Oh, dear," PZ1-3 said, and everyone looked over to him. The droid swiveled in his seat and fixed his glowing eyes on Zeen. "We heard reports that the disaster had caused severe damage to the ecology of the planet, but we had no idea of the extent of that disruption."

"What?" Zeen cried, running to the front viewport. She gasped, one hand on PZ1-3's shoulder.

Lula was right behind her. Trymant IV had been a lush forest planet, its cities perched amid towering trees and gigantic lakes; whole networks of rivers had stretched across the surface, shimmering blue veins that you could see from kilometers above.

Now it looked like nothing more than a dusty red desert.

Ram had only ever used his lightsaber in practice sessions.

He'd daydreamed about drawing it, sure. Every Padawan had. But those dreams had always seemed like far-off fantasies—tales of a world long gone, when the great wars raged between Jedi and Sith and danger lurked around every corner. These days, he'd be more likely to need his saber to fight off some wild animal than any nefarious baddies. At least, that's what he'd always thought.

But . . . the wind rushed against his face as V-18 wailed

and the speeder engine blasted them higher and higher above the trees toward three blotches rising into the sky. Three blotches that had already taken a few potshots and probably committed some kind of sabotage on the comms tower. Ram steadied the handlebars with one hand and reached for his lightsaber with the other. His fingers trembled as he wrapped them around the hilt and pulled it from its holster.

"Calm your mind, and the blade will move as part of you," Master Kunpar always said at practice sessions.

Ha. Easy to say when you weren't hurtling through the air to face an unknown enemy without any kind of backup. But that was the point, wasn't it? A calm mind was a calm mind, whether in the training hall or in battle. He took a deep breath, reached out for the vibrant tremble of the Force running through him, and ignited his blade.

FFFZZzzzzzzhhhhwwooosssSHHHHH! Ram's lightsaber sang as a bright yellow glow lit the twilight. And not a moment too soon, either. Up above, one of the figures yelled to another, and then an explosion rocked the sky.

"Incoming!" V-18 warned. Ram veered to the side just as the laser blast sizzled past, then pushed the propulsors to their limit. The one who'd fired on him had been forced to slow down to change course. This was Ram's chance. He steadied himself in the saddle and reached out with his free hand, willing the speeder up ahead to slow.

The figure on board still had her back turned. It looked like a tall Togruta woman with a gas mask on and various mismatched kinds of armor draped all over her.

Ram felt the Force flow through him, past him, and smiled slightly as it clicked with the rumbling engine of the speeder ahead. He imagined the Force sliding into the metal casing, streaming through the gears and pipes, drawing on the machine's churning heart. He closed his fist. The buzzing sound stuttered, sputtered, and then stopped completely.

Yes!

The speeder had stalled; in seconds it would plummet. Ram grabbed the handlebars again with one hand, saber still extended in the other, and gunned the engine.

"Uh, Master Ram?" V-18 muttered.

The masked Togruta turned and threw something round—a pod of some kind, about the size of a helmet. Ram watched it plummet toward the ground and land somewhere near the base of the tower with a little golden poof. Then he looked back up just in time to see the woman pull a blaster from her boot holster and point it at him.

"Master Ram!" V-18 shrieked. Ram swung hard to the side as the woman's speeder started to fall. He waved his lightsaber in a wild arc, winging one of the blaster shots and sending it off into space even as two more zipped past and a fourth slammed into his engine cover with a fizzly smack. V-18 yelped.

"Hold on!" Ram yelled, although he was the only one who really needed to be holding on to anything. The shot had jolted them to the side, and the engine was smoking but not totally busted.

The sudden roar of the Togruta's speeder filled the air. His sabotage had only been a temporary fix, it seemed. Ram looked up just as she sent three more shots his way. He deflected the first two with his saber, and the third went wide, but by then she'd sped past. Up above, a starship loomed; the other two raiders must've already boarded. The ship wasn't like any Ram had seen before—a gunship of some kind, by the size of it, with a long cockpit and a rusty, worn-out ring circling its center. The boarding ramp was lowered, revealing a gaping maw that the Togruta zipped into easily, like she was being gobbled up by a space beast.

The ship released a barrage of scattered fire toward Ram, none of it getting very close, then turned and zoomed off.

Ram squinted after it. Something seemed strange about that ring circling it. It almost looked like a—all of a sudden, the ring itself seemed to catch fire as booster blasts shot out all across it. And then, with a series of pops, the ship vanished entirely, leaving only a fading trail of engine exhaust in its wake.

"Whoa," Ram said, raising his goggles and blinking at the empty sky where the ship had just been. They were sinking slowly back toward the forest as smoke rose steadily from the shot-up engine. V-18 muttered something in a language Ram was glad he didn't understand. "Did you see that, Vee-Eighteen?"

"See us almost get murdered by a bunch of space pirates? Yes. Yes, I did. From a front-row seat, in fact."

"No," Ram said. "Well, yes. That too. But did you see that ship just make the jump to hyperspace while still in atmosphere?"

"Mm, I guess. I was busy trying not to make the jump to blasted-to-pieces space, myself."

Ram knew two things for sure:

One, it was weird for such a small, busted ship to be able to make the jump to hyperspace.

Two, even if it could, no one in their right mind would be reckless enough to make the jump from within a planet's atmosphere, risking almost certain destruction!

And those two things added up to a third, undisputable fact.

The one thing that the entire Republic feared most, the thing the Jedi and local security forces had spent months hoping to avoid, was happening: the Nihil had come to Valo.

CHAPTER

FOUR

"Wha . . . what happened here, Master Sy?" Lula asked, squeezing Zeen's hand as the transport carried them through the broken streets of Bralanak City. Zeen just frowned at the dusty glint of red sky visible through the narrow windows above them.

They'd boarded the transport in the lower belly of the *Star Hopper* and then zoomed directly out, down the gangplank and onto the surface.

Sy shook their head. "None of the larger shrapnel from the *Legacy Run* crashed here, thank the Force. Though, as you all know firsthand, plenty of smaller shards did. I checked some data as we were landing, and it seems the closest moon, a small, uninhabited one called Praknat 3, took a direct hit from the main hull of the ship, and the impact misaligned the gravitational balance of the whole system. Trymant IV tilted closer to the second sun than it's ever been, and that in turn vaporized all the aboveground sources of water."

"Wow," Lula said. "Is it still . . . can people live here?"

"They're trying," Sy said. "But I'm sure it hasn't been easy. I'd heard the Republic sent a fleet of drill freighters to search for underground water sources rumored to run beneath the lower valley area, south of here. But I had no idea how bad it was."

So much destruction, Lula thought. So many lives upended. And for what? The Nihil had caused the original hyperspace disaster, and they'd exploited it to their ends before being routed by Jedi and Republic forces. But they were still out there, being reckless and destructive with people's lives and homelands. She clenched her fists and then realized she was squeezing Zeen's hand too hard and forced herself to calm down.

PZ1-3 stepped onto the walkway. "I'm afraid I must

insist you each wear one of these." He placed a box full of breathing masks on the floor. "I know it's not ideal, given the circumstances. But the amount of dust in the air has transformed the atmosphere of the planet, and it's not entirely safe to breathe."

"Gear up," Master Sy called. "We'll have to walk the rest of the way from here."

Lula swallowed hard. She'd faced danger many times, more than most Padawans she knew. But danger was something you could face and then fight. This was something very different, and much heavier. The immediate danger had already come and gone from Trymant IV, and it trailed a long shadow of destruction and mourning in its wake. There was no enemy to confront and defeat, just the slow sadness of a world barely holding on to its own existence.

Zeen hadn't moved. "Can you do this?" Lula asked.

Zeen scowled. "You know the most messed-up part?" She picked up two breathing masks and handed one to Lula. "I don't even miss this place, not really. I mean, it's home. I spent my whole life here. But on the compound, they don't deal with moms and dads and stuff. There's just the elders and the rest of us. We don't even know who our real parents are. And sure, we're all supposed to be family, but you know . . . it's not the same."

Lula had heard her talk about this before, but it felt different now that they were back on the planet together.

"And my only friend . . ." Zeen's voice trailed off the way it always did when she talked about Krix, who had sworn to protect her and then cast her aside. That familiar sadness gathered around her, mixed with flashes of anger. Lula tried to think of the right thing to say, but Zeen looked up at her and smiled. "But now I have you all. And you're better than anything that came before." She pulled her mask on and clasped the straps beneath her gently swaying tendrils. "Now let's do this."

☙❧

Bralanak City looked like a scrap of fabric someone had crinkled up and dyed red, then tossed aside and kicked through the dirt a couple of times. Lula had no idea if they were in one of the areas she'd passed through during the rescue operation, but it wouldn't have mattered either way—nothing was recognizable. Barely anything was left.

They wound single file down an alleyway, crumbling facades and shattered windows on either side. A shredded banner flapped in the hot dusty wind, and a million tiny particles flitted through the air around them, but beyond that, not much was moving.

"Recognize anything, Zeen?" Lula asked, her voice garbled by the mask vocalizer. They sounded like the Nihil. Lula hated it.

"I think we're a little south of downtown BC," Zeen said. "Is that right, Master Sy?"

"Correct, Zeen."

"Which means the compound I grew up in should be just up . . . oh."

Everyone stopped. At the far end of the alley, a group of masked and hooded figures stood in front of a towering wall. Lula's hand went right to her lightsaber hilt. Anyone could be Nihil in these dusty streets.

"You're not welcome here, Jedi fiends!" one of them called.

Master Sy stepped forward, their robes fluttering around them in the Trymant winds. "We come in peace."

"Be gone, I said!" a short, hunched-over figure yelled, scrabbling forward. Lula drew her saber but held off on igniting it.

"Fall back!" Master Sy commanded, one hand raised. Lula knew well what that hand was capable of. With barely a second thought, Master Sy could send the attacker sprawling backward. But she also knew the last thing they wanted was to seem like the aggressor.

The hunched figure kept approaching though, howling incoherently.

"*Stop!*" came a different voice, rumbling like a far-away clap of thunder. Something huge stepped out from the shadows in front of the other masked figures. "Let me handle these intruders."

Zeen took a sharp breath. "Elder Barbatash," she whispered.

Purple and red streaks slashed the early evening sky as stars began to twinkle to life against the darkness. Ram lay on his back, allowing breath to slowly return to his body. Echoes of his run-in with the Nihil ricocheted through him, tinged with a heady mix of terror and exhilaration.

He'd been in his first real fight! He'd lived! And so had everyone else! Which was a huge relief, really. The idea of taking a life, even in battle, was almost as scary to him as the thought of losing his own. He hoped he'd never have to do it, and then, as he'd been trained to do, he did his best to release any attachment to outcomes and just exist in the gigantic spinning galaxy.

Something wafted through the air above him. It was small and trailed tiny tendrils, or microfibers, behind it. Another one floated by, then another. Ram sat up. What in the stars? A whole swirl of the specks sailed gently around him, just visible in the fading light.

They were beautiful, Ram had to admit, but something about them didn't sit right with him.

The pod the raider had dropped!

It hadn't exploded, sure, but what if it had ruptured and . . . ? Whatever these things were, Ram had to alert the other Jedi about everything that had happened, and to do that, he needed to fix the comms.

"Master Ram?" V-18 asked, blinking out of what must've been an enjoyable nap.

"I gotta see what those Nihil raiders did up here," Ram called, starting to climb up the metal ladder that ran the height of the tower. "And we gotta get you fixed up so we can get back in a hurry. If only we'd brought some of the Bonbraks with us."

"Ah, about that," V-18 said.

Ram heard the rustle of leather and then a small familiar chirp. He glanced down and yelped with joy as two tall ears emerged first and then a familiar face. "Tip! You little stowaway!"

The creature glared up at him with shiny black eyes from one of the saddlebags and squawked a long explanation that Ram didn't follow. Then two more pointy ears and another furry head poked out of the satchel: Breebak. "Man, I'm glad to see you guys," Ram said. They both scurried out, tools already in hand, and set to work squabbling and fussing with the engine attached to V-18.

The communications unit on the tower wasn't too badly damaged—just some cut wires—so it only took Ram a few minutes to replace them and restart the system. He'd tried to reach Master Kunpar and the others, but no one was answering. They were probably all at the Jedi temple already and in the midst of the opening ceremony with the Chancellor, which meant he'd have to track them down himself. Between him, V-18, and the two Bonbraks, they managed to get the engine on V-18 up and running, but it was a little janky and sputtered out every once in a while.

The sky was mostly dark by the time he rode back into Lonisa City proper on V-18, with a Bonbrak perched on each shoulder. The ceremony must've already begun; the wide avenues and winding alleyways of the Carnival District stretched on and on, empty, empty, empty. Everyone was gathered at the nearly completed Jedi temple. Banners and light displays stretched from balcony to balcony, swaying in the early evening breeze. It was so peaceful, Ram thought. Even though he didn't like crowds much, he was happy Valo was getting so much attention from the other worlds. They had always seemed so far away—impossibly far— and now they were all right there! A few kri-snorts flapped lazily toward the lake. The world, the galaxy maybe, was holding its breath, ready for the celebrations to begin.

And then, with a shriek and an explosion so sudden it sent Ram veering off to the side, they did. A huge burst of light sparkled over the rooftops: a firework. That high-pitched noise just before had been a Jedi Vector streaking across the sky. Another soon followed, along with more smacks and booms as different-colored flashes sent shimmers cascading down over Lonisa City.

The Republic Fair had begun, which meant that it would be all the harder for Ram to get to the other Jedi and warn them about what had happened. "Come on, Vee-Eighteen," he urged, kicking the propulsors into overdrive. "We gotta find Master Kunpar."

Up ahead, the tall gates of the Lonisa City zoo loomed in the shadows. Ram slowed back down as they approached. The hoots and growls of creatures from all over the galaxy emanated from behind the bars. Those chirping noises were probably the tiny night barbarbarbs, serenading each other. And that soft hooting had to be a sanval—a gigantic winged reptile that was older than time and rumored to never forget a face. A sudden, horrific screech tore the air, followed by the sound of many teeth crunching something wet and fleshy. That would be one of the hragscythe, creatures with too many claws and too many jaws, which Ram hoped to never get too close to. Sounded like it was having a tasty dinner.

He shuddered and slid to a halt, looking around for the best route to get around the zoo.

"Nrenat brak brak patak," Breebak insisted.

"The riverway shortcut?" Ram considered, then shrugged. "All right, if you think it'll get us to the temple faster." He swerved V-18 down a winding ramp that led to a pathway along the dark waters of the Karova Canal. Pleasure rafts and some security cruisers had dropped anchor along the far side, where the windows of a high-end hotel glared down at the riverway.

They zoomed under a bridge and through a creepy tunnel, then emerged alongside the scaffoldings that marked the still unfinished portion of the Jedi temple. There the four Valo Security Force gunships hovered in the air, sending their bright searchlights dancing across the surrounding rooftops, the shimmering waters of the canal, and the empty alleyways of Lonisa City. Ram ducked quickly under a dangling tarp. He shouldn't be sneaking around such a high-security area as if he didn't belong there. He was a member of the Jedi Order after all, not some intruder. But he was also pretty sure there was no other way he'd be able to get anywhere near Master Kunpar, not with all the hubbub and fanfare going on.

"Through here," he said, taking V-18 up a freight-elevator shaft. A crowd had gathered outside the temple. Ram caught glimpses of them staring intently ahead, their mesmerized faces awash in the glow of what must've been a giant holoprojection of the opening ceremony.

"Good people of the galaxy," an enthusiastic voice boomed out across the night, "welcome to the Republic Fair!"

Beyond the scaffolding, Lonisa City stretched toward the darkness of the lake in a patchwork of illuminated avenues and crossroads. The sky around the Carnival District was filled with the World Pavilions—floating islands that representatives of different Republic planets had set up to present their cultures at the fair. Each lit the night with a different color as they hovered around the main complex.

A gunship buzzed past, a little too close for comfort.

"Stay here," Ram said. He crawled off V-18 onto a scaffolding and squirmed through an opening. Down below, all the Valon dignitaries and Jedi had assembled in their finest robes. There was Master Kunpar in the middle, nodding serenely across the dais at a tall woman in an elegant cape: Chancellor Soh. Her two saber-toothed targons sat at attention on either side of her, gazing suspiciously at everyone around.

If Ram could just get down there without being spotted, he'd be able to—

"You, there!" someone with a gruff voice hollered from the scaffolding behind him. "What are you doing up here?"

Drat.

The towering creature stood perfectly still at the far end of the dusty, red-dark street.

Zeen had told them about Elder Barbatash, an ancient being who had survived some long-ago massacre and kept the dwindling light of his strange little community alive long enough to find them a safe haven on Trymant IV. She spoke about him in hushed tones and had only even seen him a handful of times. All of it made Lula imagine him as some kind of shadowy demon who haunted the edges of her nightmares.

And there he was, squinting four long-lashed eyes

against the flying particles and leaning forward on great muscled arms that extended from his tattered robes. He wasn't even wearing a mask like the others.

"You are Jedi," Barbatash boomed. "Are you not?"

Master Sy nodded. "We come only with questions. We mean no harm."

"And?"

A weighty pause extended for several moments. Lula felt the tangled grip of tension emanating from Zeen, felt it heighten till it became everything. Just as she reached out to put a hand on her friend's shoulder, Zeen stepped forward. "And I've returned, Elder Barbatash. Disciple Zeen, of the Mrala clan." She pulled her cowl back, revealing the wide halo of tendrils swirling behind her head.

Would they try to kidnap Zeen and keep her forever back in the compound? Lula tightened her grip on the lightsaber.

The elder nodded like he'd always known this would happen, but a short Zabrak beside him raised his blaster. "She deceived us, Elder! She is with these betrayers of the Force now! And it is said she herself wields—"

"Enough," Barbatash said, his voice a dull boom. "The

Jedi have been our sworn enemy for many ages, yes, but were they our sworn enemies when they saved so many of us during the disaster?"

"It was the Nihil who saved us!" another one screeched. "The Republic and their Jedi dogs just showed up to take the credit!"

"We've had enough of your shamefaced mewling, Barbatash!"

"Kill the Jedi!"

"Kill the traitor!"

"Kill them all!"

"ENOUGH!" Barbatash yelled, winding one long, shaggy arm over his head and then sweeping it down in a fierce slash that toppled all three masked men around him. Lula stepped back, eyes wide. Barbatash slammed both hands on the cracked duracrete ground, sending pebbles flying, and bellowed at the writhing figures: *"BACK INSIDE, MY INSOLENT CHILDREN!"*

They crawled off, sobbing and sputtering their apologies, and disappeared behind a gate.

The elder shook his head. "How embarrassing. They do

this more and more as our numbers and resources dwindle. Come, we have much to discuss."

※

He led them down a small side alley into a cramped room that was sealed off from the heavy atmosphere. "You look well, my daughter," Barbatash said as Zeen took off her mask.

Lula didn't trust him. Sure, he'd just intervened on their behalf, but he'd convinced Zeen to hate her own Force abilities for so long. That couldn't be any good for a person.

"I am well, Elder Barbatash," Zeen said without meeting his eyes.

Barbatash had to crouch to keep from hitting the ceiling. He gestured for them all to sit around an old table that emitted a gentle orange glow, the only light in the room. "You have questions, mm?"

Zeen nodded. "The Nihil who came here during the disaster, they took Elder Tromak with them. Why?"

Barbatash seemed to chew on the question for a few moments, blinking through memories and internal debates. Finally, he nodded. "The Nihil," he said sadly, "began as an infection, you could say, within our ranks. And when we cut off the affected area, instead of dying, it grew. It grew and spread and became many different things, chaos. But everything must return to its source, you know. Everything must return to its source."

"What does that mean?" Lula asked.

The elder fixed her with an exhausted, penetrating stare, and for a second she worried she'd spoken out of turn and somehow offended him into silence. Instead, he acknowledged the question with a shrug. "Elder Tromak was with me in the old days of our tradition. He carries with him knowledge that most don't even know to look for." He nodded, lost in memories.

"What knowledge?" Lula asked.

"The location of a very powerful weapon," Barbatash muttered. "Something that could change the galaxy forever."

A heavy silence took over the room, cut only by the howling wind outside.

"Where is Elder Tromak now?" Zeen asked. "Where did they take him?"

Barbatash shook his head. "I do not know. We only

know the location of one of the Nihil cells, and that is because one of them sent a holo back to us to let us know he is alive."

Zeen perked up. Lula felt the sudden urgency rise in her friend. "Is it—" Zeen started.

"Mmm," the Elder cut in with a nod. "Your friend Disciple Krix, yes. He messaged us from the Stygmarn system, where he said the Nihil had a base. He asked about you, Zeen, but we had not heard anything at that point, besides the rumors of course."

He'd probably been digging for info on her whereabouts, Lula thought wryly.

"Is that where they are now?" Master Sy asked, a little too eagerly.

Barbatash turned those ancient eyes to the Jedi. Then he nodded. "Perhaps."

✦

The galaxy streamed past, and then the stars stretched and spun around them as the *Star Hopper* hurtled into hyperspace.

Everything seemed to be happening so fast; Lula could

barely catch her breath. It seemed like just yesterday the galaxy was at peace and all she had to worry about was learning the skills she needed to become the greatest Jedi ever. Now entire worlds had been nearly destroyed and secret plots to bring down the Republic lurked everywhere. Combat training had always felt like a kind of meditative exercise, learned more because of tradition than any dire necessity. Padawans learned the forms, memorized each step, and honored their lightsabers as a part of themselves, and in doing so, they walked the path of every Jedi before them, and every Jedi yet to come.

But now—Master Sy took them through some exercises on the bridge as PZ1-3 coordinated with Vernestra via holo, but the familiar motions felt suddenly urgent, not just a pretty martial dance anymore.

"Dayanar Seven," Sy called, and Lula and Zeen moved as one, sweeping their arms in wide windmills and hopping backward, then pushing forward with both hands. When Zeen had first started practicing with the Padawans, Lula had felt a little bristle of irritation about it. The Mikkian wasn't a member of the Order; she was just Force-sensitive. She'd grown up hating the Jedi. It seemed unfair that she got to jump in with the rest of them. But Lula had faced that feeling and released it as best she could, and she was relieved to have her friend beside her, stepping and swinging her arms in time with her.

"Alpha-Paraval Seven." They slid sideways in sequence, then dropped into a crouch.

How many times had Lula ignited her saber to save her own life or those of her loved ones in just the past few months? She'd lost track.

But Jedi weren't supposed to have attachments, even to the past, even to a simpler, safer life. If this was the time she'd been born into, she would face it with everything she had. It was the only choice.

"I did some checking on the Stygmarn system," the holo of Vernestra announced. "There's a moon on the far edge. It's remote enough that it could be crawling with Nihil without anyone noticing."

Master Sy nodded. "Peezee, set the course. Vernestra, we'll meet you nearby and then scout from there." They glanced at the girls. "Better get ready."

"**A**h," V-18 began unconvincingly, "we are here to speak with Master Kunpar about an urgent security—"

"Security situations are the domain of the Valo Security Force," the gruff voice insisted. "And that's me: Captain Idrax Snat, of the second division." Still hiding behind a tarp, Ram cringed. Everyone in Lonisa City knew the VSF mostly just ran around pretending to be important and busting up parties when they got bored.

"And anyway," Idrax went on, "no one's allowed on this scaffolding."

"Well, I most certainly—" V-18 started.

"And why do you have Bonbraks with you?"

"I myself did not choose to bring the Bonbra—"

"There are no pets allowed on the premises, either, droid."

The Bonbraks erupted into dueling litanies of rude epithets about Captain Snat, his extended family tree, and the VSF in general. Ram only hoped the guy didn't speak Bonbreez.

No such luck. "Hey! What did you say about my grandgrub?"

The Bonbraks didn't even pause to breathe.

"That's it! You're all coming in!" A static-filled click sounded, and Idrax barked a series of codes into his comlink.

"Wait," Ram said, jumping out from behind the tarp.

"Whoa!" The captain leapt back, pulling his blaster and dropping to one knee in a single slightly clunky movement. He had the wrinkled green face and wide cloudy eyes of a Neimoidian; boney ridges lined his cheeks and forehead, and he looked like he might have never smiled in his entire life. The bulky VSF uniform made his head look too small for his body, and a bunch of probably unnecessary gear bags and canteens dangled off belts strapped across his chest and around his waist. "Identify yourself!"

Ram raised both hands. "Padawan Ram Jomaram," he said, "of the Valo Temple."

"You don't look like a Padawan!"

On that point, Ram couldn't argue. He was covered in grease and dirt. He had his goggles on and a whole tool kit with him. All the other Padawans were probably in their pristine temple attire, standing serenely at the ceremony.

"I'm—I need to talk to Master—"

"What you need isn't my concern."

The buzzing roar of a gunship's positional thrusters grew louder, and then its metallic hull rose beside them. A sliding door groaned open.

"In," Idrax grunted as the gangplank slid toward them. "You're in VSF custody now."

Yes, Ram preferred the company of mechanical doodads and electronic wiring and Bonbraks to most other sentient beings. And one of the main reasons for that was that none of the former ever manhandled you. But here he was, along with V-18, Tip, and Breebak, being gripped and grabbed and shoved rudely into a seat on the VSF ship by a Neimoidian VSF captain.

A bored-looking human in a similarly outsized uniform glanced at them from the cockpit, shrugged, and went back to fiddling with his datapad.

"I have caught some unfortunate interlopers, Officer Torgo!" Idrax Snat announced triumphantly once he'd gotten them all clamped into restraint seats.

"Yeah okay great," the pilot muttered. "Let me know when you're ready to go."

The security cushioning dug into Ram's shoulders, pinning him against the wall and making it hard to breathe. "You gotta listen to me," he pleaded. "Someone breached the comms perimeter. We might be under atta—"

"Security advice from a trespasser?" Idrax snapped at him. "I think not! Torgo, away! Bring us to the detention center."

The engine roared as they pulled off into the sky, the lights of Lonisa City spinning sickeningly below.

Ram had never been great at the whole mind tricks part of being a Jedi. Mostly because it just seemed invasive and unnecessary. But that was before Nihil raiders had attacked his planet and shot at him. Everything was different now, especially with all the most important dignitaries of the Galactic Republic gathered in one place.

If he didn't warn someone soon about what had happened, it could mean total disaster.

"Excuse me," Ram said. He locked eyes with Idrax, trying to remember each step Master Kunpar had taught him. The Force was with him. It was part of him. It flowed through him, through everything. Locking his connection with the VSF captain would be just like tapping into that engine on the raider's speeder, easier maybe. It was just a matter of using what he already knew about the machinery and figuring out the right switch to pull. "You will release me from this restraint seat."

Idrax scoffed. "I will do no such thing, you insolent slug!"

Drat, drat.

"What's that?" Torgo called from the front.

Oh, the hand wave! Master Kunpar said it wasn't

totally necessary but it did help sometimes with stubborn adversaries. Ram flailed his arm to one side, the best he could do given the security restraint. "You will release me from this restraint seat!"

Idrax blinked at him blandly. "I will . . ." His voice trailed off like he'd forgotten what he was about to say. It was working! Almost!

"You will release me from this restraint seat!" Ram said, flapping his hand back and forth a few times.

"I can't hear you!" Torgo yelled over the roar of the engines.

"I will release you from the restraint seat!" Idrax declared proudly.

"Yes!" Ram yelled. Idrax pushed a couple of buttons, and the restraint gave a mechanical sigh and lifted.

"Wait—what?" Torgo said. "What's happening back there?"

"You will take me to warn the Republic officials and Jedi about what I have learned."

"I will take you to warn the Republic," Idrax agreed, "about what I have learned."

"Er, close enough."

Torgo leaned into the back, his face concerned. "Captain? You all right?"

"To the Republic headquarters!" Idrax demanded. "Make it snappy!"

"Wait!" Ram yelped. This was *not* how it was supposed to go. But Torgo had already whirled around and pulled the ship off in a different direction. "No one's at the headquarters right now! Everyone's at the welcome ceremony where we just were!"

"To the Republic headquarters!" Idrax said again, even more excited this time.

"I'm going, I'm going!" Torgo barked from the cockpit. "Sheesh!"

Ram and Idrax's footsteps echoed down the long, empty main hall of the Lonisa City Galactic Republic headquarters. Even the custodians and security staff had headed out to catch the welcome ceremony.

"Well, here we are," Idrax said, pleased with himself. Then he paused, glancing around. "That's odd. . . . Doesn't seem like anyone's around."

Ram sighed. "That's what I've been saying for the past ten minutes!"

"Ah."

They passed vacant desk after vacant desk. At the far end of the room, a light blinked on the mainframe comms system. "But maybe . . ." Ram said, raising an eyebrow. Every Republic outpost had a direct line to Starlight Beacon. Ram broke into a run.

"Hey, wait up!" Idrax called, hurrying after him.

"Do you have the security codes to call Starlight?"

"Of course," Idrax said, looking around warily like he was waking up from a long nap. "But why would I give them to you? And why aren't you in a detention cell?"

"Uh-oh," Ram said.

"Hey, you didn't—"

"You will help me contact Starlight Beacon." Ram waved a hand past Idrax's face.

"Hey!" Idrax swatted it away.

I am one with the Force, Ram thought, narrowing his eyes. *And the Force is with me.* "You will help me contact Starlight Beacon and warn them about what I found out."

"We should contact Starlight Beacon," Idrax said. "Warn them about what I found out."

Ram nodded, quietly exhaling. "Close enough. Go ahead."

"I'll just punch in my security code here."

A holo of an elderly Dug appeared between them. "Starlight Beacon. Which area of the station are you trying to reach?"

"I'm calling to warn the Ram about what Starlight found out!" Idrax yelped.

"What?"

Ram groaned. It was going to be a long night.

CHAPTER
EIGHT

Vernestra Rwoh had light green skin and the easy, gentle demeanor of someone who had been around much longer than sixteen years. Also, she was way shorter than Lula had thought she'd be. But then, Lula was pretty sure she'd imagined the girl into a giant for no other reason than that Vernestra's very existence made Lula feel smaller. A Jedi Knight so young? It hardly seemed fair.

And even more unfair was that Lula couldn't stop this entirely un-Jedi-like thought process from cycling through her head. It felt like she was suddenly spiraling further and further from her goals, and she hadn't even had a chance to prove herself yet!

"Lula Talisola?" Vernestra said, which made Lula blink to attention.

"Yes, Master Rwoh!"

She waved the honorific title away with a soft laugh. "Please, call me Vernestra. Just not Vern. Never Vern."

Lula glanced at Master Sy for confirmation it was okay to be so casual with a Jedi Knight. Sy shrugged with a *why not* roll of their eyes.

"Yes, Vernestra!"

"You'll come with me, and—"

"I . . . I . . ." Lula stuttered. Of course she'd been too busy feeling shy and insecure to pay attention while Vernestra was running down the mission briefing. Now all she wanted to do was crawl inside herself and disappear for a few thousand years, please and thank you. "Okay!"

"Okay?" Vernestra said. "Good. You can ask me any questions you have on the way. Zeen, you and Master Sy will stay up here with my Padawan, Imri." She nodded at the tall, stocky teen at her side. "I want him to get some experience running ops from the bridge, if that's all right.

We need everyone on the *Star Hopper* to monitor any activity on the lunar surface and watch for ships coming out of hyperspace. We'll be pretty exposed down there, so if someone gets the jump on us, it'll be tough to fight our way out in that little ship. Clear?"

Once again the world seemed to have slid into some kind of raucous, sped-up version of itself. Lula could barely catch her breath.

"Clear, Master Vernestra!" Zeen and Lula yelled at once.

Vernestra nodded at Lula. "Feel like piloting?"

✦

Lula watched the mottled broken surface of Vrant Tarnum slide past as she swung Vernestra's borrowed clunker between naturally formed pillars. The *Varonchagger* handled like a rusty Old Republic tank that someone had attached wings and a hyperdrive to, but Lula was excited to get a chance to show off her piloting skills.

It rumbled and complained like an old man every time she turned too hard, like the whole thing might snap apart at any moment. "The Starlight folks really went above and beyond for you, huh?"

Vernestra chuckled. "What, ol' rent-a-junk here? Ship-master Nubarron might've been upset because I crashed my last Vector."

"Oh, wow!"

"Long story. Anyway, she'll hold up all right in a fight. Hopefully."

Somewhere within one of those canyons that snarled across the moon like a jagged gash, there was probably a Nihil outpost, with who knew how many enemy fighters ready to pounce. Lula charted how she'd slide into evasive maneuvers and then dash back to the *Hopper* if they were attacked.

"All right," Vernestra said from the tech seat behind Lula. "What do we do?"

Lula actually guffawed. "Excuse me? Aren't you supposed to tell *me* that?" The words came out before she could stop them, and she realized, too late, how rude they must've sounded. "I mean . . ."

Vernestra laughed. "It's okay—you're right. And I could

tell you, sure. But how are you going to learn if you're always just doing what people tell you?"

"I . . ."

"Exactly. So you tell me. What do we do now?"

Lula narrowed her eyes at the crisscrossing canyons. "You said the signal you picked up came from roughly this area, but it vanished quickly, right?"

"That's right."

"And you suspect the Nihil base is underground some-where." She swung lower, scanning the ground, but all she could make out were endless cracked rocky expanses and occasional calcified pillars. "So we turn our scanners on and fly low, and cover as much of this immediate area as possible to get a sense of where they might be."

"Good," Vernestra said. "And when we find 'em?"

"Blast 'em!" Lula yelled. Then, quickly: "Kidding, kid-ding." Vernestra was already laughing though, luckily. "We stay out of sight and see what we can find out, yeah?"

"Exaaactly."

Lula loved flying. She pulled the throttle and zipped through a naturally formed loop of rock, then reeled in a wide curve, letting the lunar winds dip them sideways to get a better view of the ground streaming past. Even with her mind eased, insecurities crept in. Of course Vernestra had accomplished so much at such a young age: she was the coolest person ever! And she was letting Lula run things *and* pilot? Amazing. The other Jedi had given them plenty of free rein, sure. Both Masters Sy and Yoda had sent the Padawans off on missions where they'd had to make tough decisions—life-and-death ones. But that had mostly been out of necessity, and whenever the elder Jedi were around, they were the ones who called the shots.

And then here came Vernestra, who more than anyone else had something to prove, and she had just handed over command to a Padawan.

Lula slid the *Varonchagger* so low that they skimmed just above the surface, speeder style. She spotted the charred wreckage of a small flier on a nearby hill, but other than that, the place seemed deserted. Even with Vernestra being so open-minded, Lula felt a thousand more kilometers away from her goal.

A flurry of beeps erupted from the scanner. "Whoa!" Vernestra yelped. "Powering up shields and cannons. Keep stealth mode on!"

Lula gaped at the screen, where at least a dozen dots had popped up a few klicks northwest of where they flew. She swerved low, banking behind a long rock formation, then eased the thrusters to bring them to a steady glide. A fiery burst of panic tried to rise in her, and she did her best to calm it. More dots blipped onto the screen. A lot more. The Nihil had been defeated again and again, and they kept coming back. *How?* Everyone assumed they were on the run for the most part, barely scraping by. Those ships could find them, swarm them, destroy them in seconds. "What do you think?"

"You tell me," Vernestra said, and Lula heard tension tighten her voice for the first time. "Quick."

The dots had appeared scattered at first, but looking more carefully, Lula realized they were soaring in a tangled formation. "The Nihil are on the move," she said.

"Yep." Vernestra clicked the comm. "Imri, we have movement in our sector. Keep an eye out."

"Copy," Imri's voice crackled in response.

"Now, Lula: where are they going?"

Lula shook her head and took a deep breath. The Nihil

didn't seem to be heading their way, but it was hard to tell. She checked the depth measurements on the scanner. The numbers were all going in one direction: up. The surface was point zero, and those fliers were racing toward it. "They're coming out of their hidden base."

"Yep."

"Fast."

"So any second, we should—"

"Ah, Master Vernestra," Imri's voice came over the comm. "*Star Hopper* to Jedi Master Ver—"

"Go with your message, *Hopper.*"

"We just received a transmission from Starlight. I'm going to forward it along to you so we can all watch at the same time. They said they haven't watched it all, just sent it directly to us since it mentions the Nihil and they know you're investigating them."

"Send it. And stand by for a surge of activity. They're about to—"

The first ship, a battered blockade runner, burst into the dark sky above them. The telltale external hyperspace booster formed a mechanical ring around the hull, interrupted with green half spheres of a strange design. Almost immediately, it lit up with a fierce blue light, and then the ship was gone.

A few more ships roared up behind that one, mostly single-pilot fliers of different shapes and levels of disrepair. All of them flared their external hyperdrive rings and hurled into nothingness.

"Where are they going?" Lula asked. It hadn't occurred to her that the next worst thing to being swarmed and attacked would be that the enemy just zipped away into the untraceable vastness of space. There was no way to stop them, no way to follow.

A holo popped up on the control panel, the message Imri had relayed from Starlight. A very confused-looking Neimoidian in a ridiculous, poorly fitting uniform stood beside a short human in tattered, filthy Padawan robes. The Padawan was a little younger than Lula, with a round face and light brown skin. He looked utterly fed up.

The image was scratchy, and the sound kept getting garbled, but Lula could just make it out. "And so," the Neimoidian was saying, "in conclusion, what I have seen is the why of the when where what."

The Padawan shook his head. "Ugh! We're trying to reach someone at Starlight to let you know about a possible Nihil—"

"That the comms tower has been replaced!"

"Sabotaged!"

"Sabotaged has been the comms tower! Possibly! By an unknown we don't know with a thing!"

What were they going on about? The Neimoidian wasn't making any sense, but it seemed like the human kid was trying to get him to say something. . . .

"By raiders in a ship with an external hyperdrive!" the Padawan insisted. "The Nihil!"

"I am Padawan Ram Jomaram!" the Neimoidian declared.

"No! *You* are Captain Idrax Snat of the Valo Security Force. *I* am Padawan Ram Jomaram."

"Wait!" The Neimoidian rounded on Ram, blinking his eyes like he was just waking up. "You are Padawan Ram Jomaram! And you're under arrest!"

Ram pointed at something in the distance. "Oh, no! What's that?"

Idrax Snat whirled around. "Where?"

Ram ran.

"Hey!"

The transmission cut out.

"The Republic Fair is on Valo," Lula said. "If the Nihil tried to sabotage the comms tower—"

"I didn't think the Nihil were strong enough to risk an attack on such a major target, but we gotta get to Valo now and make sure," Vernestra said. "We'll tell Starlight what we've found once we get there. For now, alert the *Hopper* to follow us and prepare to make the jump to hyperspace!"

PART
TWO

R am awoke to the murmur of a hushed conversation in the cell across from his. It sounded a little like a burbling river, he thought idly, before the realization of everything that was happening came crashing back to him. He had to get out of there! He had to warn the other Jedi that something was going on! But also: whatever those two women were discussing might be important.

"It doesn't matter," the tall dark-skinned one said in a raspy, fed-up voice. She had long light-blue hair and magenta eyes, and she wore an elaborate metal guard across her forehead that reached up on either side in two small points and stretched down around her face. "It won't do us any good to break out, not now. You want to be a wanted criminal on top of everything else, Mantessa? Believe me, it's not as glamorous as they make it look in the holos."

Ram recognized the other woman, Mantessa, as a Kuranu—she was tall and slender, and had light-purple skin that had been meticulously cleansed of even a single hair. She stood in the middle of the cell in an elegant pant-suit, glancing around irritably as if a germ or spot of dirt might jump up and attach itself to her at any moment. "Nobody's going to put *me* on a wanted list, Ty. Don't be ridiculous. And anyway, the whole thing was a misunder-standing. Clear it up with your Jedi buddies and let's be on our way. There are deals to be made, hm? And anyway, we have to find Klerin."

"They're *not* my buddies," Ty muttered.

Across the room, a security droid stared at a control panel, occasionally hitting buttons. He probably had keys on him, Ram figured. If he could just . . . He reached out with the Force, feeling along the control panel and desk and then the length of the droid.

"Tried that," the Tholothian woman, Ty, said gruffly. "No good."

Ram sat up, blinking through the bars at her. "Oh, you're . . . you're . . ." *Your Jedi buddies*, Mantessa had said.

"I'm Ty Yorrik," she said. "That's all I am."

"You're not a Jedi?" Ram asked.

Ty smiled. "Not today, no."

"Ty works for me," Mantessa said with a huff. "Her one mandate is to keep me safe. She's doing an abysmal job of it so far."

He waved. "I'm Ram. I'm a Padawan here on Valo."

"Looks like you had quite a night," Ty said, eyeing his grease-stained robes.

"Oh, no—I mean, yes, but I always look like this. Er, not for important events and stuff, but I mostly work in the garage, so." This was another reason why Ram didn't like being around people: he had to explain himself and try to make things make sense, and it was, quite frankly, exhausting and a waste of time.

"Well, you'll be disappointed to learn they've really upped their security here because of the fair," Ty said. "It's surprisingly well locked down for such a rinky-dink little holding area."

"Thank you!" the droid chortled obnoxiously from his control panel. "I am Five-Triad, security protocol droid in charge of this facility. Welcome! And yes, we have upgraded everything to the most cutting-edge security technology! Can't have anything go wrong, you know!"

"See?" Ty snorted.

Ram walked to the edge of his cell and grabbed the bars. "That's the thing though! We're about to be attacked! You gotta let me—us—out!"

The droid threw his long head back in an awkward mockery of laughter. "Ha! Attacked! Okay, 'Padawan.' I'm so sure."

"It's true! Raiders sabotaged the comms tower last night before the welcome event! I think they were Nihil."

Mantessa shot him a sharp glare. "Don't be ridiculous, child. Everyone knows the Nihil were all but destroyed months ago. The ones left wouldn't dare attack such a—"

"How do you know this, kid?" Ty interrupted, striding past her patron to face Ram from the edge of her cell.

"Because I stopped them! Well, me and Vee-Eighteen and the Bonbraks. They had ventilator masks, and their ship jumped to hyperspace before they cleared atmo! I swear!"

"This is a fairy tale," Mantessa spat. "Jedi aren't supposed to lie, you know."

"I'm not lying!" Ram insisted. "And if they attacked the comms tower, it's probably part of a larger plan! We gotta—"

"Well, whether he's lying or not," Ty said in that quiet growl, "we all want the same thing, no?"

"Why don't you two do your little Jedi mind tricks on that droid and let's be on our way then, hm?"

"I'm right here, you know," 5-Triad pointed out.

"Our mind tricks don't work on droids," Ram said, trying not to sound too irritated. "Which is probably why they left one to guard us."

"Exactly!" 5-Triad agreed.

"It's true Jedi mind tricks don't work on them," Ty said.

"But this does." With a squeal the droid shot up into the air and smashed into a light fixture. Ram ducked as sparks and smoke poured out of the droid's crumpled head.

"Ow!" 5-Triad moaned, still dangling from the light. "That wasn't very Jedi-like!"

"Fortunately, I'm not a Jedi."

"Is that going to get us out of here?" Mantessa sputtered.

Ty shrugged. "Probably not, no."

"Then—"

"He was irritating me."

The droid finally came crashing back down and landed in a sparking heap. "I will personally see to it that they add five years to each of your sentences, you barbarians."

"Would you stop messing around and get us out of here?" Mantessa roared.

A dull boom sounded from somewhere nearby. Then another, so close that the whole building shook. Ram looked around. He heard people screaming outside, and then he heard the sudden shriek of blaster fire.

The attack on Lonisa City had begun.

CHAPTER
TEN

The stars streamed past, the galaxy a blur once again.

Would things ever slow down? Lula wondered. They'd jumped to hyperspace, and the *Star Hopper* was probably right behind them. They would emerge into some kind of mess about to unfold; that seemed sure enough. And Zeen and Master Sy would be thrust into danger, and who knew what was going on with Farzala and Qort and the others.

Lula knew she wasn't supposed to form attachments, and she understood why—she could feel it jangling up her flow, twisting her connection to the Force into unintelligible knots. But what else was she supposed to do? She cared about her friends and didn't want them to get hurt.

And Vernestra looked so calm there in the tech seat, like they weren't rushing into yet another disaster. No wonder she'd already been knighted at such a young age. How did she do it?

"What is it?" Vernestra asked over the quiet hum of the engine.

"What's what?"

"Come on, Lula. We're both Jedi. Don't make me explain what I already know you know. Your heavy thoughts are taking up more room in this little ship than you are."

Lula scrunched up her face. She should've known her own thoughts would betray her, especially around such an on-point Jedi Knight. "How did you do it?"

"Ah, you know we don't get into details of our final trials, Lula. I'm sorry. But also . . . that's not really what it is you want to know, is it?"

For a few moments, Lula just let the stars whoosh past. "As Jedi," she finally said, "we're not supposed to be attached to anything, right?"

"That's the idea, sure."

"But . . ." Lula suddenly felt like a dam was about to break. She realized she'd never had anyone more advanced than her to talk about this with. And even with the other Padawans, no one wanted to admit what they struggled with, deep down inside. "I'm like . . . just a big huge ball of attachments!" she moaned. "I'm attached to being alive! And to my friends being alive, too! And to Master Sy! Every day I go somewhere new in this galaxy and feel attached to it, meet more wonderful people that I don't want to be hurt or killed! The attachments just keep coming! If I live to grow old, I'll have thousands and thousands of them! I'm even attached to the *Star Hopper*, and that's just a silly ship! Ugh!" She wasn't sure if her voice was wavering with laughter or tears by the time she was finished—it felt so good and terrible to get it all off her conscience, *finally*!

But it didn't change the fact that she couldn't manage the most basic thing about being a Jedi. "I'm such a failure," she said, rubbing her eyes.

Vernestra's small, strong hand slid along Lula's shoulders and squeezed. "Ah, Lula. Not at all. You're so strong."

"I am?"

The Jedi leaned forward so her head was beside Lula's.

She was smiling. "Of course! Being a Jedi isn't about not having feelings or caring about anything. You know that."

"I do?"

Vernestra laughed. "If Jedi weren't supposed to feel *anything*, we might as well be droids. And even they feel things, if you think about it. The fact that we feel, that we care, is what makes the Jedi great."

"But—"

"Balance," Vernestra said. "Being a Jedi is about balance. Balance of the Force within you, the Force in the wider world. Balance of the Force as it flows through us." Her voice was calm; she seemed so sure of what she said.

Would Lula ever feel that certain about anything? "Balance," she repeated, trying to sound confident.

Vernestra smiled. "Take Master Sy, or your friend Zeen. You would try to save them, if their lives were in danger, yes?"

"Of course!" Lula said. Master Sy was one of the people Lula loved most in the whole world. And Zeen . . . Zeen seemed to understand Lula better than anyone else, even though they'd led entirely different lives up to this point. Opposite lives. She would do anything for her friend.

"But a stranger, or an enemy even," Vernestra countered. "You would save their lives, too, or no?"

Lula felt like she was walking into a trap, but she tried to answer as honestly as possible. "I would, yes . . . especially if they weren't trying to kill me at the time."

Vernestra let loose a sly smile. "Ha. Smart answer. But you don't care about them, right? And yet you'd save them anyway. Why?"

"Because I care about life. And the light. I'd save them because it's the right thing to do."

"And that is also why you'd save Master Sy or Zeen. Let me ask you this: If saving Master Sy or Zeen meant that you'd never see them again but you'd have the knowledge they'd be safe, would you still do it?"

Lula almost yelled, "Of course!" but something inside made her hesitate. She wanted to be sure it was true. She'd be heartbroken never to see Master Sy again, but she knew it'd be a thousand times worse if it was because they were dead and she'd let it happen! The same was true of Zeen, although the ache at the idea of not seeing her friend felt momentarily like it would overwhelm her, an emotion so big she didn't have room for it in her body.

It didn't matter. The answer was the same, and she was already beginning to see the truth Vernestra had been trying to light up for her: that her actions, her choices, revealed the deeper balance that being a Jedi required. It didn't mean cutting yourself off from love or not having emotions. It meant finding balance within those emotions to be able to still seek out the light, to do the right thing.

She nodded. "I would."

Vernestra looked pleased, and Lula felt a swell of pride. "Then you are saving them for them, Padawan, not for yourself. It is not attachment.

"Speaking of not being attached to things, switch spots with me. We're about to come out of hyperspace, and I need you on guns, just in case."

Lula stood and let Vernestra slide past her into the pilot's chair. Then she plopped down in the gunner's seat and started checking the equipment.

The ship was definitely a clunker. The scanner screen had to be a few decades old—chunky blips danced gracelessly across it, leaving behind little phantom versions each time they moved—and the laser-cannon turrets, visible on either side of the spherical cockpit window, swiveled on rust-covered rotary hinges, never quite catching up to where they should be.

"We'll let Starlight know what the situation is once we know what we're dealing with," Vernestra said. With a blip and a rattle, they jolted out of hyperspace, the whole ship jiggling and creaking, and zoomed closer to the green-blue planet below.

Lula had to breathe through a wave of nausea as the stars shifted and slowed around them. "Ay, ay, ay, ay," she moaned with the starboard engine's grunts. "Whew!"

As soon as everything came to a gradual rest, lights erupted across Lula's target screen.

"There is an attack!" Vernestra yelped, tilting them forward. "And it's already begun! Alert Starlight!"

Up ahead, hundreds of ion trails roared to life as Nihil fighters streamed in reckless, chaotic swooping dives toward Lonisa City. Down below, blaster fire ripped across building tops, floating pavilions, and crowded streets, and bursts of smoke plumed into the sky.

Only static came over the comms when Lula tried

to raise Starlight. "Comms aren't working!" She tried the *Hopper* and got the same result. "And I don't see any Republic ships. Is it possible they don't—"

"No time to work out why. Do your best to get a distress signal to Starlight," Vernestra said. "We're going in."

Lula tried, but the system kept sending back an automated message in a language she didn't know. "I thought that Padawan said he'd fixed the comms tower. It doesn't seem like—whoa!" She almost choked on her own tongue as Vernestra hit the boosters, rocketing them toward the swarm.

"All weapons live!" Vernestra yelled. "We need to punch a hole in this pack to throw off their attack pattern!"

Lula opened her mouth to object, or plead for a moment to catch her breath, but they didn't have that luxury. Innocent people were being massacred on Valo, casualties piling up with every passing second. And already they were roaring up behind the attacking horde.

"Fire!" Vernestra called, her face scrunched with concentration.

Lula brought the control grips to rest on the two crafts

closest to them, then pulled both triggers. Blaster fire splattered out from the turrets in an angry blitz of light, shredding the hyperdrive of one ship and lancing through the rear cannons of the other.

Vernestra dipped the *Varonchagger* slightly to one side, clipping two smaller crafts with its bulky wingspan. They spun into a cluster of three more ships, and the lot of them burst into flames, spiraling out of the sky.

But the other Nihil had realized there was an attack from their rear, and several swung their ships out of formation, whipping upward and back around with laser cannons blazing.

"Hold on!" Vernestra hit the thrusters hard and spun skyward, past the attacking raiders, then cut off all the thrusters. The *Varonchagger*, convulsing angrily with one hit after another, sank suddenly.

Lula met the goggled stare of a Nihil raider in a single-pilot craft bearing down on them, the swirl of space behind him. He lurched forward, blasting his wing cannons. She swung the turrets in a diagonal swath across the sky and released a barrage of laser blasts that carved through four

Nihil ships. Then she concentrated both cannons on the approaching raider. Smoke and flames burst from his cockpit first; seconds later his whole ship disappeared in a fiery explosion that sent shards cracking against their front viewports.

The man was dead, Lula realized, blinking. She'd killed him. She'd been in battle before, had taken other lives, but it never got easier.

"No time for that," Vernestra said, sliding her hand over Lula's. "Not right now. After the battle, we must process, heal, rebuild. Right now we have to give our time only to making sure we get out of this alive."

Lula nodded. Already, more Nihil ships zoomed toward them, and Vernestra was angling the *Varonchagger* to meet them head-on. "You're not scared?" Lula asked.

"Oh, I'm terrified," Vernestra said with a nervous little laugh. "But this is what I mean. . . ." She swung the ship suddenly sideways, then sent them in a spiral over a forested expanse outside the city—leading the raiders away from the populated areas, Lula realized. "Balance. If we're not scared at all"—she grimaced as laser fire rattled across their rear and starboard shields—"we can't be courageous, right? And we might make mistakes in our arrogance. But if we're overcome by terror, we'll be useless, too."

"I guess," Lula sighed. She switched to the side cannons, bringing up a static-laced image on her screen and swinging the sights into place on the swarming attackers. "I mean, I'm trying." She let loose another barrage of fire, but the Nihil seemed infinite—four spun out of the sky in flames, and seven more took their place.

Vernestra swung them back around over a gorgeous lake that Lula thought would be a very peaceful sight in other circumstances. Fighters and puffs of smoke filled the sky over Lonisa City. From down below, thick green-yellow clouds of that nasty chemical gas the Nihil used rose over the buildings at various points around the city. An urgent alarm rang out. "Shields are about to—" Lula started, but another burst of fire shook the *Varonchagger*, and more beeps erupted.

"I know," Vernestra said through gritted teeth.

A group of Jedi Vectors screamed up from the rooftops, the first sign of a counterattack. They must've been on the planet before the attack began. Lula exhaled, then squeezed the triggers on the rear cannons and shook her head. "There's too many!"

"I'm bringing us down," Vernestra said.

"On purpose?"

"Something like that."

The sun-sparkled waves seemed to roar up to meet them. Ahead, a sandy embankment led up to a boardwalk, where riotous crowds ran every which way.

"Hold tight!" Vernestra yelled.

The Nihil who had been pursuing them must've realized they had bigger problems to deal with—they shrieked off overhead toward the air fights erupting with the Vectors.

The *Varonchagger* skimmed the top of the lake, then bounced once, and again. Vernestra swung them into a hard turn, sending out a massive wave of water and sand. Finally, they slammed to a teeth-chattering stop along the embankment.

"Another one!" Vernestra was already out of her seat and heading for the exit. "Shipmaster Nubarron's never gonna forgive me for this!"

Lula hurried after her. "Wait! What do we do?"

A purple glow lit the dim interior of the *Varonchagger* as the crisp sizzling growl of a lightsaber sounded. Lula's wide eyes tracked a long, slender stream of pure power as it bristled and slid through the air around them. It was a lightsaber, but now it was also a whip. "I've never seen anything like it," she whispered.

"Don't tell anyone, okay?" Vernestra allowed herself a slight smile. "You have yours?"

"Of course, but—"

"It looked like that Padawan who sent the message was getting arrested, so he'll probably still be in the local lockup. It should be one of the domed buildings in the center of town, Government District. Break him out and find out what else he knows."

"What are—"

"I'm going to find the elder Jedi and make sure the Chancellor is safe. The comms might be down, but it could just be interference from everything going on. If not, you'll need that kid to help you get them back up. Got it?"

Lula blinked, then steeled herself. Somewhere out there, Zeen and Master Sy were probably having a similar conversation. They were in danger, all of them, and the knowledge of that rippled through her with a shudder. But she had to stay focused. She had to do whatever she could to get everyone to safety. She nodded once as the blue light of her own saber blended with the purple glow of Vernestra's. "Let's go."

"Look, kid," Ty said as the sounds of fear and battle outside raged ever closer, "things are about to get messy."

Ram nodded. Mantessa was fussing with some small bit of tech she'd stashed away, but whatever she was trying to do didn't seem to be working. The droid, 5-Triad, bustled back and forth, pushing buttons and yelling nonsensical commands, oblivious to his crushed head.

"Can I count on you?" The rogue Force-wielder's raspy voice was strangely kind, calming even.

Ram wasn't sure if he was up to the occasion—he'd

only just been in his first fight a few hours earlier, after all—but something about Ty Yorrik made him want to step up and get it right, whatever it took. "Yes," he said, hoping he sounded more assured than he felt. "Tell me what you need."

"That'll depend on—"

The prison door slid open, and a sizzling fusillade of blaster fire exploded into the room. The droid flew backward with a shriek and landed in a smoldering heap. "Unnecessary!" he warbled as a tall, muscular man with a cannon-sized blaster stomped in. His gas mask had three eyestalks built into it, which meant he was probably a Gran. "Mm, Jedi?" he yelled, voice distorted. He raised his weapon. "We'll see about that!"

"You will retrieve our things and release us from these cells," Ty said firmly, with the slightest wave of her hand.

The Gran cocked his head at her, nodded. "I will retrieve your things and release you from these cells," he agreed.

"And then you will subdue and capture any of your fellow Nihil that you find."

"And then I will subdue and capture any of my fellow Nihil that I find."

"Whoa," Ram gasped.

The raider crossed to the far end of the room, where a passageway led to the storage area, somewhere deeper in the complex.

"Zarabarb!" someone with a gruff voice yelled from outside the door. "What are you doing, man?"

Ram cringed as the Gran spun around, blaster cannon already raised, and unleashed a devastation of laser fire that tore half the wall to shreds. Something heavy fell to the ground in the other room, but more shouts were rising now, and Ram heard boots stomping toward them.

"That's a very creative interpretation of *subdue*," Ty muttered. "But oh well." She glanced at Ram. "Get ready to improvise."

A few shots zinged through the shattered opening where the door had been, then something flew into the room, clinked a few times on the ground, and rolled to a stop.

"Thermal detonator!" Mantessa yelled.

Ram had already reached out with the Force and felt his connection click onto the orb. If he sent it out into the hall where it came from, it would probably kill whoever was trying to kill them. But what if other people were out there—hostages or prisoners? It was too risky. He sent it zinging past Zarabarb's head and straight out a window. A sharp crack followed, shattering the other panes.

"Minimal damage to the enemy," Ty commented. "But otherwise not bad."

"Charge!" someone yelled, and a group of Nihil burst in, blasters blazing.

Zarabarb clipped two of them before charging into the fray and lashing out wildly with his huge arms.

"Push them back!" Ty ordered. Ram imagined the Force gathering into an unstoppable wall as they both raised their hands, then shoved forward. With a yelp and a clatter, the entire tangled brawl of Nihil flew backward, smashing into desks and data-comps.

"Ha!" 5-Triad yelled from somewhere underneath them. "Take that, villains!"

Ty gave a gruff nod of approval, then growled. "Blasters, quickly now."

This was trickier. Some had fallen in the tangle; others were still gripped in sweaty hands. Ram reached out with the Force, felt the cold steel of those weapons, and pulled with all his might. Several slid across the floor toward him as another group hurtled through the air and clanged against the bars of Ty's cell.

A twitchy gnaw of tension in the Force made Ram look up to where a Mon Calamari Nihil had crawled to his feet, a bowcaster raised in his long webbed fingers. It was pointed right at Ty. Ram narrowed his eyes. If he tried to yank it away from the raider's tight grasp, it might not work in time. Instead, he sent his mind surging through the greasy steel valves and gears of the weapon. It was different than anything Ram had seen before, but he quickly made sense of the machinery. With the slightest nod of his head, a spark leapt up, then a crunch. "Gah!" the Nihil yelled, dropping the bowcaster and leaping away as smoke poured out of it.

"Not bad," someone snarled. "Now put your hands up!" Ram looked across the room to where a tall, purple-skinned woman stood with a shoulder rifle aimed directly at him.

"I—" Ram started, but then the woman flew backward with a grunt as a laser blast slammed into her.

He glanced over at Ty, who had pulled one of the Nihil's blasters through the bars of her cell. A small plume of smoke slid up from its business end.

"Argh!" the Mon Calamari yelled, charging at Ty and then collapsing in a heap when she blasted him once and then again.

"Sweet dreams, sweet seafood," she said with a smirk.

"Whoa," Ram said, mouth gaping.

Ty rolled her eyes. "They're just napping. Now . . ." She pointed her blaster at a control panel on the other side of the blasted-open door, squinted, and let off one shot.

With a wheeze, her own cell door slid open.

Ty winked at Ram. "Teamwork! With a Padawan! I'm almost as impressed with myself as I am with you." She headed for the hallway. "Now let me get yours—" Ty raised both hands and took a few steps back, that slight smile still on her bemused face. "Well, well, well."

A purple blur burst past her into the room. Something short and furry rode on top. Two somethings. Bonbraks!

"Vee-Eighteen!" Ram yelled as the droid jolted to a stop and glanced around. "How . . . ?"

Then Ram saw the bright blue tip of a lightsaber, followed by its owner, a girl a little older than him, in Padawan robes, with a very severe frown directed, along with her lightsaber, at Ty Yorrick. "Drop the blaster."

Mostly, people in the streets had stayed away from Lula. She'd been scared—terrified really—about being alone out there. It hadn't occurred to her just how used to her Padawan squad she'd become until she had to face down an enemy without them. But she quickly learned that the Nihil hadn't come expecting much resistance; most traveled in groups of two or three, and once they caught a glimpse of her lightsaber, they gave her a wide berth and slinked off to hunt easier prey. There wasn't much coordination to their attacks, either; it just seemed like a terrifying free-for-all.

Even at the detention facility, the two raiders posted out front scattered quickly as she approached. But this Tholothian woman, who didn't appear to be a Nihil, was another story. Even as she retreated, hands raised, and put down her blaster, she looked like she'd somehow won.

"It's okay," the Padawan in the cell said anxiously. "She . . . helped me!"

Lula glanced over at him. Ram Jomaram, the kid who'd sent the message. He was short, a year or two younger than her, and a bit of a mess, all in all—still in grease-stained clothes, with his hair all disheveled. He'd had a rough night, of course, but Lula had the feeling this wasn't an unusual state for the kid. The outpost Padawans really did lead very different lives than those more closely tied to Starlight or Coruscant, she realized. "You trust her?"

The woman leveled an intense magenta-eyed stare at Lula.

"Yes, uh, this is Ty Yorrik," Ram said. "She has the Force! And that lady is Mantessa Chekkat."

"You're . . ." Lula looked at Ram. "She's not a Jedi."

Ty rolled her eyes. "We don't have time for this right now. Let us go."

She was right; they didn't have time. But that didn't mean they should just be letting criminals escape from jail, especially Force-wielding ones. What if this woman was part of the attack? "Why is she in here in the first place?" Lula asked.

Ram shook his head, eyes wide. "I don't . . . Lula, I might be dead without her."

"Get out of the way immediately, girl!" Mantessa demanded in a haughty growl. The woman was middle-aged and dressed in elegant finery that spoke of important meetings and negotiations. Her tone was that of one who does not take being told no lightly. "This is no time for foolery."

Lula stepped past Ram to face Ty directly and looked up into the warrior woman's fiery eyes. Her mind was reeling. "You . . . you left the Jedi Order?" It was more of a guess, really, but the way Ty's face seemed to tighten ever so slightly made Lula pretty sure she was right.

"Listen, kid: any second a whole bunch more Nihil are gonna bust through that door, and it's gonna take more than two Padawans to hold them off. Ram already told you I helped him, and you saw the mess these guys were in when you got here." She nodded at the bedraggled crew on the ground. "There are a lot of things out there more important than your precious Jedi Order, and staying alive should be number one on that list."

For a smooth couple of seconds, they just stared at each other. Why would anyone with the Force leave the Order? It seemed incomprehensible to Lula; it would be like chopping off your own arm. But she believed Ram—he probably wouldn't have been able to subdue all those Nihil on his own, and it was clear that Ty Yorrik was very powerful with the Force. . . .

Mantessa stepped forward, and Lula saw something in the older woman's eyes—desperation. "My . . . my daughter," Mantessa choked out. "She's . . . she's out there, in all that. I need to find her."

Lula glanced at Ty, whose stern face revealed nothing. Neither of them seemed particularly trustworthy, but Mantessa wasn't lying, that much Lula was sure of.

One of the Nihil snorted from the ground. "If it were up to me—"

Ty silenced him with a single move of her hand. She hadn't used the Force to do it, just the sheer ferocity of who she was.

"It's not."

"All right," Lula said, exhaling. It felt good now that the decision was made. Whatever happened would happen, but this wasn't a fight she needed. She extinguished her saber. "But if it turns out you lied to me, I'll come find you. Don't think I won't just because I'm young."

Infuriatingly, Ty unleashed a sly smile and raised her eyebrows as she and Mantessa walked past. "So I see, Padawan."

When they'd left, Lula reached back to the panel in the hallway and opened Ram's cell. "I'm Lula Talisola," she said when he walked out, brushing himself off. "I'm a Padawan, too. You okay?" She patted him on the shoulder, hoping it would seem reassuring. Outside, the sounds of fighting rose and fell amid the ongoing carnage of Jedi Vectors and Nihil raider ships clashing overhead.

Ram nodded, then shook his head, and finally just shrugged. "I don't know. What's happening? How did you find us?"

"Starlight relayed your message to a Jedi Knight I was with, Vernestra Rwoh. We were investigating the Nihil, and as it turns out . . . they were on their way here. We don't know the whole story yet, but we've got to . . ." She waved her hands helplessly as the full scope of whatever it was they had to do loomed impossibly huge, incomprehensible.

"We've got to get my stuff and get out of here," Ram said, already heading down the hallway to the storage area.

Lula followed. Once they got away from the detention center, they could meet up with Vernestra and find out where Zeen and Master Sy were, and then . . . well, that was a lot, really. And anyway, it felt like they all might get incinerated at any moment, or overrun by a Nihil horde, the way things were going.

"Here it is!" Ram said, pointing up at a box on a cabinet. He pulled a metal ladder over and started up it.

Lula pulled out her comlink and clicked it. "Vernestra? Come in, Vernestra."

Only static came back.

"What is it?" Ram asked from above.

"The comms from our ship." Lula shook her head, then

tried again. "Vernestra? Can you hear me?" She frowned. "It's still not working. That's why I came to find you."

Ram looked stricken. "The tower . . ."

"You said you stopped them from attacking it last night?"

He climbed down with the box. "Yeah, they'd sabotaged it, but I fixed it, and . . . it had to be working because my message got out to Starlight, right? That's how you all got here."

"Yeah," Lula said, "but it wasn't clear what was going on. They just knew it was something to do with the Nihil, so they sent it to Vernestra. That's why we came. But if comms are down again, that means—"

"No one can coordinate a counterattack on the ground," Ram said.

"There are some Vectors in the air that must've been here already, but nowhere near enough." Lula shook her head. "And no one's coming to help us."

CHAPTER THIRTEEN

R am had been feeling a rising rumble of inse-curity since seeing how poised and powerful Ty was, and it only got louder when Lula showed up. As a Padawan at one of the Republic outposts, Ram didn't come into contact with other Force users much, besides the other Jedi in his temple. And they mostly left him to his repairs. Anyway, no one was that competitive on Valo; folks just went about their business. But now . . . the wider galaxy had opened up suddenly and violently in a matter of hours. Ram's whole life had been Jedi studies, things he had to fix, and Bonbraks. It had been going back and forth from the under-construction temple to the living quarters to the lake, and one or two trips offworld at most. And up until now, he'd figured that was what his life would always be, for better or for worse. He'd grow old here on Valo, like Master Kunpar, and one day take on a Padawan probably—hopefully one who loved to fuss with mech stuff and didn't talk much.

But now, as they stood in the battered detention facility listening to chaos and battle sounds rise around the city, *his* city . . . the only thing Ram knew for sure was that nothing would ever be the same.

He took a deep breath. *You must see the whole for the whole, and each part for the role it plays—not for what you want it to be, not for what you fear it to be. Just for what it is.* Whatever happened next, this moment was a crucial piece in it all, and he and Lula might be able to do something good amid so much destruction.

"I know what we have to do. We have to make it back to the tower. Whatever they did when I caught them out there yesterday—there must've been more to it than just sabotaging the comms right then. They must've . . ." Those swirling pods in the setting sun . . . What if they had something to do with it?

"C'mon," he said, placing Breebak and Tip on V-18 and climbing on. "We gotta get back out there now!"

Lula gaped at him. "What, on the droid?"

"Oh," V-18 said haughtily, "Breebak and Tip and I have been working on something while you lot were relaxing!"

Since when had V-18 even gotten along with the Bonbraks? Now that Ram had a moment to look him over, he realized the droid had a whole different engine welded onto him. And was that a small starfighter propulsor?

"*I* haven't been relaxing!" Lula said. "And I don't think sitting in a jail cell qualifies as—"

"*Fitzabom takna takna!*" Tip insisted.

"They upgraded the old speeder engine I had retrofitted on there," Ram translated, helping Lula climb on. "To something a little spiffier."

"You put a speeder engine on a droid?"

Ram shook his head. "Long story."

"ENGINES FULL POWER!" V-18 announced.

Breebak squealed with delight. Tip muttered something rude.

"Uh," Ram said. "That might not be the best—"

Tip let out a wild yodel as they zoomed through the blown-up wall, then into the war-torn streets of the Government District. It was a bright sunny day, one that would've normally sent Valons out for a splash in the lake or a stroll along the boardwalk. Instead, flaming debris rained down from the starfighter clashes above and screams rang out amid blaster shots all across the city.

At the far end of the street, a crowd scattered past, stumbling and limping, and then about a dozen Nihil raiders stomped into view, swinging clubs and spears. A tall one with six arms turned his masked face toward Ram and the others, then yelled something.

"We've been spotted!" Ram said.

"Already?" Lula said. She'd maneuvered around in the seat with her back to Ram's so she could keep an eye out for anyone chasing them. "Which way to the tower?"

Ram reeled V-18 around. "At this point, any way will do! We just gotta—"

"Incoming!" Lula yelled as they sped away.

Ram heard Lula's lightsaber shriek to life. He wasn't sure what he was supposed to do—speed up or veer off or just stay the course? One wrong decision could mean they all ended up roasted. "Incoming *what*?"

"I'm on it!" she yelled as the roar of approaching speeders grew suddenly louder.

"OH, THESE SNOGGLE-MASKED MUSKWORTS WANNA PLAY?" V-18 yelled.

"Uh, what's going on with your droid?" Lula asked.

"I'm not su—"

"VEE-EIGHTEEN IS TIRED OF BEING SHOT AT!"

Ram cocked his head. "Did he just refer to himself in the third person?"

They veered into a tight U-turn, and something whirred and clicked into place beneath them.

The Nihil apparently didn't care what V-18 was tired of: the six speeder bikes had pulled up to a halt and all ten raiders were raising their blasters.

"*Fatoopa fatoopa fatoopa!*" Tip yelped.

Ram translated: "Apparently they also installed a—"

Cannon fire thundered out, shaking the whole block and bursting in riotous explosions across the buildings and pavement around the Nihil. The raiders dove for cover; most of their bikes burst into fiery ruins.

"Weapons system."

"Wow," Lula said.

"Fatoopa," Breebak agreed solemnly.

Already, a few of the Nihil were standing, dusting themselves off, and grabbing their gear.

"Now we go!" V-18 said, spinning back around.

They jolted forward, zooming around a corner and then weaving among a few scattered people in the street. Two speeders raced along behind them, and Ram could hear the pairs of Nihil on each one yelling back and forth.

A bolt of light flew by, smashing with a fizzly explosion into the wall nearby. "They're closing," Lula warned. "Hold steady." Ram felt her shifting on the seat. Was she— He glanced back. The girl was definitely raising herself into a wobbly standing position even as more blaster shots screamed past.

"COMING THROUGH!" V-18 hollered. A Gran lunged out of the way. "WOOT WOOT!"

"I guess if he's gonna drive," Ram grumbled, "I can . . ." He managed to turn around and pulled himself into a squat. Lula swung her lightsaber once, batting away a blaster bolt, and then again, smacking another. Her face was calm but determined, like she'd been training for this moment her whole life. Which, Ram realized, they both had, really. But he felt somehow totally unprepared anyway.

Behind them, the pursuing Nihil speeders blitzed through the street, knocking over anyone who got too close. The nearest one was about to pull up alongside them. Lula knocked away one more shot, then crouched low and leapt onto the front steering vane.

"Whoa!" Ram said, igniting his own lightsaber, but he barely had time to pay attention as Lula slashed the shooter's rifle in half. The other speeder was coming up fast and had a rapid-fire weapon system on board. The air exploded with laser blasts. Ram swung his saber left, right, and then in a wide circle in front of him, sending one shot after another ricocheting into the walls around them.

Lula had knocked both Nihil off and taken over driving the first speeder, but the ones on the speeder shooting at Ram had pulled up alongside hers and were trying to shove it into a building.

"Vee-Eighteen, keep us steady!" Ram yelled, feeling

the droid wobble beneath him. He reached out with the Force and felt the vibrating rumble and heat of the Nihil speeder's engine.

"I AM KEEPING STEADY!" V-18 snapped back. "But there's something up ahead I can't make out."

"Huh?" Ram couldn't look or he'd lose the hold he had on the engine. "Hang on!"

Lula slashed at the attacking Nihil speeder just as it swung out of the way. The rider fired two shots at her, which she deflected quickly, but Ram could tell driving with one hand and fighting with the other wouldn't work for long.

He refocused on the engine, blocked out everything else, and used the Force to shove it into overdrive.

"Ayeeee!" yelled the Nihil in back as smoke poured out around him. He leapt off the speeder with a shriek, but the one driving must've hit the accelerator in his panic—the speeder dipped forward, and the directional rudder scraped against the street, snapped in half, and sent the whole thing cartwheeling forward in a fiery explosion.

"Watch out!" Ram yelled as flame and debris burst toward Lula.

She glanced to the side, then took her speeder roaring upward, over the tumbling disaster. A fireball clipped her rudder though, and she threw herself off the seat, then somersaulted once on the pavement and leapt up running.

"Um . . . up ahead!" V-18 warned.

"You okay?" Ram reached out to Lula as she caught up to them. "What is it, Vee-Eighteen?"

"Just cuts and bruises," Lula said, grabbing his hand and hoisting herself up. She'd snatched a satchel off the Nihil speeder, Ram realized, and must've slung it over her shoulder before the wreck.

V-18 made a concerned whirring noise. "That seems bad."

Ram whirled around. Up ahead, a dense greenish-yellow fog rolled closer and closer.

"**C**an we go around?" Lula asked. They'd pulled up to a hover right in front of the dense fog. More blaster fire and screaming emerged from within, along with a few other ominous noises—growls and moans—that Lula didn't even want to guess the origin of. She'd been through the Nihil's horrible chemical attacks before, and she never wanted to be anywhere near them again.

Ram shook his head. "This is the only way to Crashpoint Tower."

"Crashpoint?"

"That's just what we call it," Ram said. "Folks like to practice speeder maneuvers up there. Doesn't always go well. Anyway, let's go!"

Lula steeled herself. At least with V-18's upgrades, they could zoom through fast—or fast-*er* than walking, anyway—and be on their way. She handed Ram the satchel she'd grabbed from the Nihil speeder. "Put one on."

He pulled out a rubbery face mask with various gaskets and tubes on it. "Whoa! Good thinking!"

Lula managed to find a smile somewhere amid all the fear and turmoil. "I've faced off with these raiders before, unfortunately. I spied this while we were tangling on the speeders and figured they might come in handy. They sometimes keep one or two size-adjustable ones in their jump bags, so maybe we can find something for the Bonbraks."

"Ah, I have more bad news, in case you were looking for some," V-18 said.

"We weren't," Lula and Ram both snapped.

"Wow, touchy. You're welcome for saving your lives with my fancy new upgrade, by the way."

"Thank you," Ram said unconvincingly. "What's the bad news?"

"I think I'm leaking?"

Ram and Lula both slid off the droid and peered underneath, where a shiny black puddle was spreading quickly below a burn-bruised slash in the engine. "You've been shot!" Lula yelled, stepping back. She wasn't expecting it to affect her so much, but the droid had indeed saved them, even if he'd copped an attitude about it. And it was just one more terrible thing in the midst of so much awful. She looked at Ram. "What are we going to do?"

He glanced around the deserted street, surprisingly calm, then nodded at the two furry creatures poking their heads out of one of the saddlebags. "Can you guys get him up and running?"

Breebak and Tip leaned over from their perch to get a good look at the damage, then they conferred in quiet chirps. Finally, the taller one turned his huge black eyes to Ram and nodded once. *"Ponk."*

"I shall place myself in the noble wizened hands of these eloquent creatures," V-18 proclaimed. "Go on without me!"

"We'll keep moving." Ram pointed to a back alley stretching off into the shadows nearby. "Take him in there.

And when he's back up and running, head to the comms tower. We'll probably need a hand. Or . . ." The fact that Ram and Lula might not make it there hung heavily in the air.

"Affirmative!" V-18 said, already making his way to the edge of the street. The Bonbraks fussed about something then waved goodbye.

"Thank you!" Lula called. "For helping us! Be careful!"

She traded nervous glances with Ram. "On foot?"

"That's the best way for now," he said grimly. "I'm not sure how long that repair will take, so we're better off going ahead while they work on it."

"But . . ." Something about that fog. It wasn't just that she'd been in a Nihil-generated fog before and never wanted to be again—a vicious kind of seething emanated from it this time, like some horrific creature lurked within. Whatever it was, though, they'd have to face it. There was no other way. Lula pulled her mask on and nodded at Ram, and together they walked in.

"Does the Force work on it?" Ram asked as they stepped gingerly down another cobblestone street amid a seemingly impossible mustardy cloud.

Lula shook her head. The Nihil mask barely fit. The straps pulled at her braids, and its rubbery edges gnawed at her flesh every time she moved, but better too tight than too loose. "A little, but not enough to be worthwhile for all the effort it takes to clear an area."

They didn't want to light their sabers—it was too risky, with innocent people running around, and anyway it would draw more attention than they were looking for. So instead they just walked very close to each other and cast wary glances to either side as they went.

"If we keep going down this street," Ram said, "it'll lead us along the edge of the lake and then into the outskirts, and finally the woods. Problem is, it'll also take us through—"

"Halt!" an angry voice called up ahead.

Lula and Ram stopped in their tracks. That restless, sinister seething feeling still pulsed outward from somewhere nearby; in fact, it had gotten stronger. But they had other problems to deal with. A Nihil raider stepped through the fog, blaster rifle pointed directly at them. Two more followed, and five behind those. All of them had their weapons trained on the Padawans.

"Jedi!" the leader said. The others muttered back and forth and advanced on either side of him. "Drop your sabers!"

Lula didn't know Ram well enough to be able to game out what he'd do, but she hoped he'd at least follow her lead. There were more of the Nihil, sure, but she still had her weapon. Giving that up would mean giving up the whole fight, and she wasn't about to do that. Her saber ignited at the same time as Ram's, and she smiled inwardly.

"They're gonna attack!" someone yelled. "End them!"

Blaster fire blazed everywhere; Lula and Ram swung and swung, backing up side by side, step by step. A few Nihil dropped, winged by their own deflected shots, but the others kept advancing.

"What were you going to say we had to go through?" Lula asked as she batted away another shot and then another.

"Oh," Ram said, spinning his own lightsaber in a wild windmill motion. "The Lonisa City—"

That seething feeling suddenly reared up from the mist just as a horrible screech sounded up ahead.

"Zoo."

"What was that?" Lula gasped. The Nihil stopped shooting and glanced around. There was nothing to see, though; their own chemical attack was unyielding.

Ram stepped backward, pulling Lula with him. "Sounded like a—"

With a clang, something large and metal flew out of the emptiness and skidded along the street: the busted-up entrance gate to the zoo. Two long, sinewy arms emerged from the fog. They ended in clawed feet that cracked into the pavement where they landed. The screech sounded again as the creature's face appeared, long snout opened wide in four directions to reveal glistening, blood-soaked teeth and six squirming tongues. Then a second and third head emerged. A half dozen eyes glared out in every direction behind all those gnashing jaws.

"Hragscythe!" Ram finished. "Run!"

Lula took a few steps back as the hragscythe advanced, pounding one clawed foot after another into the pavement— she counted six total. The Nihil turned their fire toward it, but they were too late; it was already on them. The first three were swept away by a vicious swing of its front claws. The rest scattered, screaming, but the hragscythe snapped up one in its gaping maw and clobbered another with a strike of its long spiny tail.

Lula turned, saw Ram's lightsaber glistening through the fog ahead, and ran.

"They can breathe this horrible stuff?" Lula asked as they ran side by side through the fog.

"Apparently so!" Ram yelled. He was running out of breath and answers. There were so many things he'd realized he didn't know about the world in the past couple of hours, he'd lost count.

"It's coming," Lula panted. "I can feel it!"

They both whirled around, lightsabers lit, but the fog remained a thick and impenetrable wall around them. Footsteps approached at a run, and Ram raised his lightsaber. By the time the Nihil emerged into view, just a few meters away, the hragscythe was already on him, that vicious face appearing just above and then swooping down to grasp the raider and yank him screaming into the fog.

"I don't think we can outrun it!" Ram said as they ducked around another corner. "This way! I think!"

He led them down a ways, but he wasn't totally sure where they were anymore—the whole world had become a mist-covered nightmare. A rumble came from up ahead—not explosions, though, something huge running toward them. Ram put his arm out, stopping Lula in her tracks as another Nihil squad appeared out of the mist, looking around. They heard that low thunder, too, felt the ground beneath them tremble.

"More Jedi!" one yelled, spotting Ram and Lula.

"Wait!" another called before they could open fire. "Over there!"

The Nihil all raised their weapons and started shooting, a barrage of different kinds of blaster fire that flashed into the heavy fog and then seemed to be swallowed up by it.

"Ahhh!" someone yelled, and then a Nihil went flying over everyone's heads and landed in a heap nearby.

"Run!" the others yelled, scattering into the mist. A gigantic beast stomped forward with an uneven gait.

"It's the mudhorn!" Ram yelled. It was coming right for them, head bowed low so that gigantic horn on its snout would drive right through whoever it hit. "We gotta get—"

Ram didn't finish, because the mudhorn seemed to look directly at them and run even harder. A Gungan Nihil ran by, firing his blaster in all directions, and the mudhorn clipped him with one shoulder as it stampeded past, sending the raider flying off into the mist.

Lula stepped forward, face determined.

Ram reached for her. "What are you—" But the mudhorn was almost upon them, and closing fast. Lula raised one open hand, thumb over her heart, palm facing to the side, edge to the approaching beast. She moved it sideways toward her shoulder, and the mudhorn moved with it, stumbling, eyes wide with confusion. It tripped and crashed forward, tumbling sideways with a grunt and then sliding into a storefront, which shattered.

The beast scrambled to its feet and lumbered off into the mist.

Ram shook his head. "Whoa!"

"Do you know how we can get out of here? Because we'll never make it to the comms tower at this rate."

"I do have a thought, actually." The idea had been growing since they'd rounded the corner. Lula was right. They could barely even get a block without being shot at or almost eaten, and even if they could, there was no way to navigate through this fog. How did the Nihil manage it? Ram wondered. It didn't matter; if he and Lula couldn't see through it, maybe there was another way. . . . "Follow me."

Ram leapt onto a parked speeder, then flung himself upward through the fog, grabbed hold of a flagpole, and used it to vault to a third-floor window ledge. There he waited until Lula caught up. Then he nodded at a balcony jutting out above them, and together they jumped, clutched its railing, and hauled themselves up.

Already the mist was thinning out. They could see almost across the street, and up above it looked even clearer. They heard a starfighter zoom past, followed by the screech of cannon fire that flashed red through the fog.

"Brilliant," Lula said, and Ram felt a surge of pride. "Let's keep going."

They worked their way higher and higher, bouncing

from window ledges to balconies. By the time they climbed onto the rooftop, the sky was clear around them.

"Oh, no," Lula said, taking her gas mask off and walking to the edge.

"What is it?" Ram ran up beside her, unstrapping his own mask. "Oh . . ."

The city Ram loved and had grown up in was in shambles. Most of the Carnival District and a huge stretch of the Government District were steeped in that horrible fog. Smoke rose in billowing towers from all across the building tops, and the screams of scared people sounded from the streets below. Out over the lake, the floating pavilions swarmed with signs of destruction. A few listed dangerously; others had caught fire. Speeders zipped away in all directions, desperate to escape. The biggest pavilion, which they'd all revolved around—the one representing Coruscant—was simply gone. Blasted out of the sky probably, taking with it untold lives.

A badly burned transport poked from the surface of the water—the *Innovator*, Ram realized with a gasp. Chancellor Soh's flagship. A battle seemed to be raging on top—Jedi lightsabers flashed as Nihil blaster bolts were flung back and forth. Ram couldn't make out anyone he knew from where he stood.

Up above, Nihil fighters streamed through the sky, dancing and dangling in the air. A squadron of Jedi Vectors flashed past, blasting a few of the Nihil crafts to pieces, some getting clipped by return fire.

Lula wrapped her hand around Ram's. It wasn't just his own world that was ending, that would never be the same—even if it felt like it looking out over the ruins of his home city. No, an attack so bold, so relentless, so devastating could only mean one thing, and Lula knew it, too: the Nihil had never been truly defeated. They'd been lying in wait, biding their time. This wasn't some singular sleeper cell of troublemakers; this was an all-out assault on everything the Republic stood for, on the Jedi themselves.

But also, Valo was being destroyed before Ram's very eyes, the people of Valo slaughtered mercilessly. All that pain and terror swept over him in a wave, and he didn't even realize he'd been crying until Lula reached over and wiped one of his tears away with the sleeve of her robe.

"I . . ." he started to say, but no words made sense. Instead, he let Lula wrap him in a hug and hold him close while he released all that fear and despair.

"We have to . . . do something. . . ." He sniffed. "We have to help them." There were so many hurt people, so much fear. It felt like the fabric of the Force itself was trying to rip in half in the air around them.

"We have to get to the comms tower, Ram," Lula said firmly. "That's what we can do."

"But . . ." He reached out a shaking hand to the burning city, then let it drop. She was right. Everything in him wanted to swoop down into the streets, whisk everyone to safety one by one, and fight off all the hordes of Nihil. But they would never be able to help everyone, and they'd probably get killed in the process.

No. He had to see the whole for the whole, not get distracted by each part. The whole of this wasn't one attack on one street corner; it was the entire city. More than that, Ram realized, it was the whole Republic under assault. If the Nihil carried the day, if they were allowed to simply sweep in and massacre all these people with no one coming to help, no one even trying to stop them, beyond the Jedi already there, well . . . then it was open season on the galaxy. Anyone could do anything.

The Republic needed to know what was happening; they needed to send help. And for that to happen, the comms tower had to be up and running. At least it was something Ram could actually do, was good at even.

He wiped his eyes and took a deep breath. "If we go rooftop to rooftop, we can make it to the lakefront. From there it's not too far to the edge of town."

Lula nodded. "Let's do this."

PART
THREE

CHAPTER
SIXTEEN

Zeen Mrala.

Farzala Tarabal.

Qort.

Lula ran across the uneven gravel of another Valon rooftop, stepped up onto the short wall at its edge, and leapt.

Master Sy.

Master Yoda.

Vernestra Rwoh.

Each step was another name; each name was a prayer. She sailed through the air over a small side street, ignored the fighting below, the sounds of yelling, blaster fire, explosions.

All that mattered was each moment as it came—the rooftop swinging up to meet her, her boots landing on the ledge, her legs bounding across it, Ram up ahead leading the way. Each moment, and each friend she held dear to her heart and hoped was okay as the galaxy fell apart around her.

Ram led her along a narrow walkway between two buildings, then around a shining dome. A burning starship careened past and exploded in a park nearby.

Balance, Vernestra had said. Balance.

There were so many lives at stake, so many already lost. Lula had to stay focused. But the names kept cycling through her mind, even as she hurdled across a wider avenue, lost her footing on the far ledge, and slid down, saving herself only by grasping a stone gargoyle.

Zeen Mrala.

Farzala Tarabal.

"Lula!" Ram called, gaping down at her from above.

Qort.

"I'm okay!" she yelled, though her fingers were slipping.

Master Sy.

Ram was already climbing down the wall. "Hold on! I'm coming!"

Master Yoda.

"No!" Lula insisted. "I got th—"

The gargoyle cracked and leaned dramatically forward, and then Lula felt the wind swoosh up around her as she plummeted.

"LULA!" Ram threw his arm up over his head, and Lula was suddenly swinging through the sky, toward the wall. She landed on it feetfirst and ran upward as the gargoyle smashed into the pavement below and shattered.

Lula pulled herself onto the rooftop with a groan. She was on her feet and dusting herself off when Ram reached her, panting. "You okay?"

She blinked, still reeling, then nodded. "You saved my life."

He waved her off. "Ah! I just gave you the assist—you did all the hard work."

She looked around, her heart finally slowing as the burn in her scraped palms seemed to roar to life. She had to focus. Yes, balance was possible. And right now balance meant not being attached to outcomes she had no control over. Especially because the one she *could* do something about was so important.

"You ready to keep going?" Ram asked. "We're getting close to the—"

The drone of an engine revved into a sudden roar, shaking the rooftop they stood on. Lula and Ram whirled around as a bulky class-three asteroid hopper sank out of the sky until it was eye level with them.

Lula could make out the horned head of a Devaronian inside. A grinning human woman sat beside him. The ship had a spherical cockpit up front and two bulky wings stretching to either side. A whole battery of cannons peered out from each wing.

"Down!" Lula yelled, tackling Ram as she lunged for the ground. Laser fire splattered across the rooftop, singeing the air just above where they huddled. At the first pause Lula stood, lightsaber extended, and braced herself for the next round of firing. It would only take one deflected hit, angled just right, to take out one of their engines or a wing. She could do this.

Ram got to his feet beside her—unhurt, thank the Force—and lit his own saber.

The attack never came.

Instead, a high-pitched caw sounded, and a long shadow swooped across the rooftop where they stood.

Lula squinted up just in time to catch a flash of purple scaly flesh and two immense wings swinging overhead and then barreling directly at the asteroid hopper. The creature wrapped its long muscly tail around the ship and yanked it backward. Lula barely had time to react to the spray of laser fire that erupted in an upward arc from the wings—the gunner must've panicked. She and Ram raised their lightsabers just in time to send each shot blitzing into the rooftops around them.

The cockpit window cracked, then shattered completely, and the huge flying lizard spun upside down and whipped the wrecked ship straight up into the air, then swatted it once with its tail, demolishing the whole thing. The flaming wreckage smashed into a building and then clattered to the street below.

Lula realized her mouth was hanging open. The serpent

swung into a graceful arc above them and landed with a mighty thud a few meters away. Someone was riding it, she could now see. A woman.

"Greetings, Younglings," Ty Yorrik said, sliding easily off the creature and stretching her shoulders like nothing particularly exciting had just happened. She had an impressive gilded face guard covering her mouth and chin, and Ram noticed she'd gotten her lightsaber back.

"We're Padawans, not Younglings," Lula said, caught somewhere between amazed and slightly annoyed.

"Yeah, yeah. I brought you a gift."

"Is it your flying serpent thingy?" Ram asked a little nervously.

Ty let out a raspy, humorless chuckle. "Heh. No."

Another shadow passed overhead, this one much bigger. "It's her mom."

A s it turned out, Ty Yorrik had brought them two surprises. The mysterious Force user took off on her own ride as the gigantic sanval landed on the rooftop with a skull-rattling thud, those long claws carving deep gashes into the tarmac. Ram took a few steps back—he knew it was exactly what they needed to get to the tower, but also: yikes.

Lula gave a gasp of joy, though, and ran forward.

Ram realized this sanval had a rider, too—a girl Lula's age with magenta skin and slowly swaying tendrils on the back of her head—a Mikkian. "Zeen!" Lula yelled. "How—"

The girl flashed a winning smile and shrugged. "Master Sy and I were fighting off some Nihil by the main pavilion, and we helped this Ty here out of a jam. She offered to help me find you."

"Is Master Sy—"

"They're okay!" Zeen said. "Headed off to help protect the Chancellor." She extended a hand and helped Lula up.

"This is Ram," Lula said, settling into place behind Zeen. "He's a Valon Padawan. He knows where the comms tower is and how to fix it, so we're heading out there."

Ram tried to smile and do what he thought people were supposed to do when they met someone new, but he wasn't even sure what that was. And anyway, what if he couldn't fix the comms? Or what if something else had gone wrong that they didn't even know about? Amid everything terrible going on, the sudden pressure to live up to expectations felt impossible. "Hey," he said with a wave he was sure was awkward.

"Good to meet you," Zeen said, and Ram could tell she meant it—she didn't seem like the type to say things idly. "I'm Zeen Mrala. You coming?"

"Uh, yeah! Definitely!" He approached cautiously,

excruciatingly aware of the giant sanval head looming over him, that humongous forked tongue sliding from one side to the other.

He took Zeen's outstretched hand and tried not to act shocked when she scooted back so he could take the frontmost spot. The sanval smelled like soil and swamp; her muscular shoulders swiveled beneath Ram, and then the creature lowered and burst upward into the sky.

"Yeeeeeep!" Ram yelped before he could stop himself.

"I know! It's wild, right?" Zeen said with a nervous laugh. The rooftop spun away below them, and within seconds the whole city spread out on either side and the sky, still torn by smoke and starfighter fire, became their world.

"How do you . . . ?" Ram started, but what was the word? *Drive* didn't seem right. "Ask her to go in a particular direction?"

Zeen laughed. "I haven't been, to be honest. Ty whispered something to her and told me to get on, so . . . I tried reaching out with the Force, and it kinda worked. Like, she wanted to hear me."

"Oh, you're . . ." She wasn't wearing Padawan robes, but she just said she used the Force. Anything he said after that would sound rude, so he was relieved when she answered his unasked question anyway.

"Not a Padawan, no, but I roll with Lula and her crew."

"Long story," Lula said. "We'll tell you when we all get out of this alive."

Ram liked the idea of them sitting around and having an easygoing conversation when they were safe. He wasn't sure if they'd all survive, though. So many already hadn't.

Below, the city gave way to shimmering lake and then forest. He closed his eyes, reaching out to the gigantic sanval with the Force. He felt a surge of energy rise within him, like she understood, so he imagined the route through the trees to the comms tower.

"Uhhhh, company," Lula said.

Ram glanced back, and his heart sank. It wasn't just a fighter or two—what looked like an entire Nihil cell spread out behind them, and it was closing fast.

Worse than that, though, the fog they'd had to fight through back at the zoo—the Nihil's chaotic battle tactic of choice—was rising over the building tops, so it looked like the whole of Lonisa City was being consumed by a giant smoke monster.

The Nihil were taking over.

And without any way to coordinate a response, the Republic and the Jedi couldn't strategize a meaningful counterattack.

Hurry, Ram urged, and he was pretty sure the wind whipped harder against his face and the trees blurred past even faster.

"How far?" Lula asked.

"Should be just . . . over . . . this . . ." And sure enough, they crested a small slope, and there was the open field by the tower. Except . . . "Oh, no," Ram said. "What happened?"

The tower still stood, which he at first thought was a good thing, but green shrubbery had grown almost halfway up it. Worse—the plant seemed to be writhing along the tower legs. *Growing!*

This must've been what was in that pod the Nihil had dropped the night before. They'd taken out the planet-wide comms, but they knew someone would probably be able to fix them. So they'd left behind a time bomb, basically. One that would sprout and grow and take over Crashpoint Tower entirely by the time the attack was in full swing.

A group of Valon Security Force troops must have had

the same suspicion. They approached the plant-consumed tower at a brisk jog, weapons out, then halted a few meters in front of it and consulted with each other.

Whatever kind of plant it was, that movement was more than just rapid growth, Ram realized—more than just a plant's natural sway with the wind. No . . . that thing wasn't any regular plant. It was a creature.

A long tendril bristling with huge, razor-sharp spines whipped out suddenly, just as the first VSF trooper charged toward the base of the tower. Another tendril swished through the air, then another. They converged above the trooper, who didn't seem to notice them.

"That thing, it's . . ." Ram gasped as they sped into a dive toward the tower. "It's . . . it's . . ."

"Drengir!" Lula yelled.

The spiny tendrils swung down, two scooping up the trooper and yanking him toward the brambly mire while the third slashed at the group standing back. They scattered, sending blaster shots in all directions.

The trooper was gone.

rengir!
And they'd already devoured at least one Valon.

Lula had heard about the malicious sentient plant creatures that seemed to be spreading around the Outer Rim planets like a carnivorous weed. Farzala and Qort were even now off with a Jedi expedition to destroy them at their root. But those sinister vines wrapping around the comms tower could mean only one thing: the Drengir had allied with the Nihil. And that was bad news for everyone.

Worse still: they had some twisted connection with the Force that no one seemed very clear on. Whatever it was, it was the dark side, of course. Lula could feel the cold, cruel energy coming off of them in waves. It felt like a dirty sponge being wrung out inside her, and all she wanted was to get away.

"I'll hop off on that platform," Ram said as the sanval swooped in a low circle, "and see what I can do about fixing it." From his gritted teeth, Lula could tell he felt that nastiness, too.

"Those plants," Lula warned him, "they won't let you near it. You saw what they just did to that trooper!"

"We have to do something," Zeen said. "I'll go with him and hold them off while he does what he has to."

"But . . ." Lula had hoped she'd have Zeen to help her fend off the fast-approaching Nihil ships. It wouldn't be easy to take them on single-handed. But if Ram wasn't able to get near that control panel, there was no point in any of this. The sanval slowed at the uppermost platform of the tower, above the writhing branches of the Drengir.

Lula nodded. "You're right." She met Zeen's eyes. They'd only just found each other again amid this disaster, and already they had to part, each to face off with something that wanted them destroyed. It wasn't fair. *Balance*, Vernestra's faraway voice echoed within. The Force was about balance. And Lula would need all the balance she could get to defeat these raiders. "May the Force be with you both," she said.

Ram and Zeen nodded and leapt from the sanval's scaly back to the platform.

"Let's go," Lula said, forcing herself not to watch her two friends descend toward the Drengir.

The sanval glided in a long, languorous spiral upward. The creature moved through the air like it was water— tiny flinches of her muscular, serpentine body sent her listing to one side or the other, and huge swooshes of those four gigantic wings blasted her forward like a giant scaly torpedo.

Lula didn't know what Ty had told the sanval, but she could feel the huge lizard's hunger for chaos, destruction, explosions. "Okay, girl," she said, patting the cool hide beneath her. "Soon enough."

Out over the trees, the Nihil ships had fallen into a holding pattern. There were about ten of them; most buzzed around in small circles while others hovered in place, but none got too close to the clearing.

That's odd, Lula thought, even as the sanval launched toward them, huge jaws wide to release a triumphant roar. There were so many of them. Why would they— "Wait!" she yelled, placing her hands on the sanval's huge neck to get her attention. "It's a trap!"

The sanval's desire to destroy thrummed and shrieked like an electrical current in the air around them. "Wait!" Lula pleaded. She wasn't quite sure what the trap was yet, but she knew something was off. And rushing into the attack was exactly what the Nihil wanted her to do.

"Swing back around," Lula said. "There'll be plenty to destroy, mama, I promise."

The sanval turned so suddenly that Lula almost slid down those smooth shoulders and tumbled to her death. She saw the first ship burst up over the treetops ahead as she was adjusting her position. Another came soon after it, then another. She narrowed her eyes. The group behind her had been waiting there to lure her attack. That would've left Ram and Zeen defenseless, especially since their hands were probably full with the Drengir right about then.

Three more ships rose over the forest, and all six blasted toward the tower. They were small single-pilot fliers—nimble and fast, probably with precision firepower but nothing too heavy. If they'd wanted to destroy the tower, it would be gone already, so clearly they were invested in protecting it. The Drengir were just there to temporarily knock out the comms during the attack, and the Nihil would probably repair them once the Republic reinforcements had been crushed, use them to call their own backup.

At least that meant they wouldn't blow up the tower with Ram and Zeen on it. But they also wouldn't hesitate to take shots at them if they had the chance.

They wouldn't get the chance, though; Lula would make sure of that.

Down below, she thought she caught a glimpse of her friends making their way toward the tangled leaves and vines. She couldn't make out much more than that. She'd just have to trust that they'd be okay and do what they had to do.

Up ahead, the small Nihil crafts were almost at the clearing.

Behind her, the engines of the other ships revved. They

would probably come zooming over now that they'd real-ized their little ploy had failed.

Soon she'd be totally outnumbered.

Lula took a deep breath, the understanding of what had to be done taking shape.

No point in tackling the whole galaxy herself when she had such an eager helping hand available.

"All right, mama," she said, patting the sanval lovingly and guiding her into a steep climb. "Just swing us right up top of those ships ahead. Then you do whatever you need to with the ones behind, okay?"

A thunderous growl that reverberated all the way through Lula was the only reply. Lula smiled. It was the right one. Down below, the first Nihil craft spun toward them, a few blasts zinging past.

Lula eyed it, timed it, and, as they flew over, slid off the sanval, saber lit, and let the air take her.

CHAPTER
NINETEEN

"Ummmm . . ." Ram said, eyeing the tangle of spiny creatures a few meters below. It was hard to tell, but it looked like there were eight or nine of them, all wrapped in a deadly labyrinth around the tower pillars. "What are these things again, and why are they here?"

Zeen laughed, which Ram realized was a nervous habit, not an actual expression of joy. He'd have to remember that. "Drengir. They've been causing trouble around the galaxy recently. A bunch of Jedi just rode out to face their main hive on the edge of somewhere. They hate everything that's not them, from what I understand. And they eat . . . like . . . uh, people."

"They eat people?" Ram boggled. "They're plants! And do they make an exception for, like, the worst people? They're here doing the Nihil's bidding aren't they?"

Zeen shook her head, still chuckling through gritted teeth. "No idea, man."

"MEAT!" a voice like curdled milk came from below.

Ram lit his saber. Zeen pulled out two blasters. "This is why I prefer machines," he said with a scowl. "They don't try to eat you."

"MEAT MEAT MEAT!" The vines and branches, which had been creeping and crawling toward Ram and Zeen at a gradual rate, suddenly lurched closer. Huge, razor-sharp spines poked out of the thick stalks as they stretched upward, wrapping tightly around the metal legs of the tower.

"We don't want to hurt you!" Ram yelled, edging lower stair by stair. The control panel was half a level down, only a few more steps. "We're just trying to get to that comms box, that's all!"

"This meat is talkative!" one Drengir commented.

"Talkative meat is often quite chewy, I find," another noted.

"Has fancy light sword, mm?" said a third.

"Ahh, those meats are especially testy."

"But also succulent, I have heard!"

A collective "Mmmmmm!" rose up.

Ram took a few more steps and heard Zeen close behind him, felt her shivery breaths and the bristling of her fear as it rippled through the Force and mixed with his own. "Hello? Are you even listening to us? I'm talking to you! I don't want to use this light sword, okay? We're not trying to hurt you!"

The Drengir rose all around them, their wooden, leafy tendrils clasping and creaking as they stretched and twined ever upward, blocking out the treetops and sky.

"Do you speak meat?" one hissed.

"Of course, we are speaking it now! I find it dull, though. Try to ignore, mostly."

"I, too. A useless skill, really."

"Ram . . ." Zeen said.

"I know, I know." They'd reached the box. The front

casing had been popped open, and a thick vine snaked through the middle. "Drat."

"How bad is it?" Zeen had her back to Ram, facing the swarming plant creatures around them.

"It's bad," Ram said. "I might still be able to fix it though. I just need time. . . ."

"Is time to eat, then?" a Drengir whispered.

"MEAT!" they all cried at once. Rustling erupted from everywhere.

"I don't think we have that!" Zeen said, and laser fire burst from both her blasters, shredding through the plants closing in on them. The charred stumps recoiled, revealing a brief glimpse of the blue sky, a group of approaching starfighters, clouds. Flaming leaves and twigs rained down around them as Ram pulled out the damaged wires from inside the box and clipped off their twisted ends. Zeen stopped shooting, her breath heavy.

"Wow! Meats with an audacious and ferocious desire to remain uneaten," a Drengir mused. "It is interesting!"

Ram secured the fixed wires in the remaining slots, slid a shattered pulse node out of the way, and clicked the outlying modulator bracket back into place.

"Back!" Zeen yelled. The Drengir had already begun regenerating; a cruel chuckle rang out over the rustle of leaves. "Stay back!"

Ram scowled. Those blasters weren't going to hold the Drengir off for much longer. He ignited his saber and sliced away the chunk of vine still sticking out of the comms box. Then he deactivated the blade and reached over his shoulder to tap Zeen with the hilt. "We're not really supposed to share them," he said, "but we don't have much choice. You may not be an official Jedi, but I know you have my back, and anyway, I need your help!"

Zeen blinked, eyes wide, then beamed at him. She holstered her blasters and took the lightsaber. "Thank you."

"Meats share bright weapons!"

"Hold them off," Ram said, turning back to the box. "We'll need all the help we can get."

Drengir were crowding in from the far side of the platform, chuckling and chatting rudely with each other as they went. Ram extended his hands, palm out, and used the Force to push them away, then got back to it. Zeen grunted as she cleaved a vicious swath of open space around them.

"Ayeeeee! Feisty meats!"

"Meats and meats!"

More sizzling branches and leaves collapsed around them.

Ram had cleared all the debris from the box, fixed the wiring, and gotten the sensor systems up and running. All that was left was to connect the main transmission vortices, but those were closeted away in the rear area of the system. . . . He popped open the little door protecting them and groaned. The main vortex was shattered, and all the smaller ones were dangling out in a tangled mess.

"Bad news," he called over the swoosh-swoosh of his own lightsaber chopping back and forth.

"I got some of that, too," Zeen said. "You first."

"We're missing a crucial piece of this comms unit. What about you?"

"These plants seem to grow back faster and faster every time you chop them."

Ram spun around. Zeen had been keeping a good stretch of open space around them, but already the sky was blotted out again by rising branches. "Yikes."

"Also, I think their spines are getting bigger."

"Meats!"

"Prepare to eat meats!"

"What do we do?" Zeen asked, her wide eyes finding Ram's.

Ram shook his head. He had no idea. "Keep fighting."

Lula slammed down on the roof of a single-pilot craft with a thud. She landed in a squat, making sure the impact didn't reverberate all the way up her spine, both hands out for balance. The ship swerved suddenly to one side and Lula threw herself down and grabbed a gun turret to keep from flying off.

Her lightsaber flew free from its holster and into her hand, and in seconds it was lit and burning a bright gash into the starboard thruster engine. That ought to do it. Lula pulled herself up, one hand still clutching the cannons, braced herself, then leapt away just as it nose-dived toward the treetops, smoke pouring out of it.

She landed on a passing pocket cruiser. The long, fast ship had been modified so its main-cabin canopy could roll back when it wasn't in deep space, making it look more like an elaborate speeder. Four Nihil raiders were crammed inside—one driving, two with their blasters out, and the fourth behind a rear double-laser cannon. Lula scurried up the long nose cone, dodging from one side to the other as blaster shots zinged by. She leapt over the windscreen, came down solidly on top of the pilot's helmeted head, threw an extra knee drop in for good measure, and then sprang forward, flipping over the other raiders, and slashed the double cannon down the middle as she slid to a stop on the rear ion accelerator.

The Nihil behind the cannon tilted his masked head at her for a second, bewildered, before they all turned and screamed. A small fighter blitzed toward them, lasers blazing. Up ahead of Lula, a single Nihil raised the top hatch of what looked like an ancient escape pod that had come to a hover. He pulled out a shoulder-mounted torpedo launcher.

A barrage of fire from the fighter, an R-wing, slammed into the mini cruiser, sending it listing to the side as a few of the raiders dove for cover.

Lula jumped.

The trees were a blur below, the wind a furious shriek in her ears.

She was one with the Force and the Force was with her. She felt it rise inside her.

But she wasn't going to make it. The escape pod was too far. She'd already hit the highest point of her bound and was starting to descend.

With all her might, she used the Force to pull the pod sharply downward, even as a torpedo surged toward her. She swatted the missile away with her lightsaber and grabbed the bottom rung of an exterior ladder on the pod, swinging up fast so she wouldn't get singed by the low sizzle of thruster fire.

"Hey!" the Nihil on top yelled, glancing around for her. "Where—"

But Lula had already scrambled up the side and pulled herself onto the lip of the opening. It just took a small shove with the Force to slam the top hatch shut on the raider, who dropped his launcher with a yelp and collapsed inside.

Lula stood and surveyed the battlefield around her.

The empty mini cruiser sank in a flaming, smoky dive toward the treetops, felled by the fighter's attempt to blast Lula off it. The first ship she'd landed on had already crashed, and the pod she stood on was out of commission.

The three remaining ships circled above, reassessing who they were up against, no doubt. They let off a few shots, which Lula easily batted away. Out in the sky toward Lonisa City, the sanval had sent a few fliers careening toward the ground, but she was chasing a larger vessel that had made a break for the main battleground.

The other raiders had already turned their ships back toward Lula and were approaching quickly.

How much longer could she hold out? She glanced down, saw flashes of blaster fire and the shine of Ram's yellow lightsaber swinging amid the tangled Drengir, but she couldn't make out anything else.

Up ahead, the Nihil ships were already launching a fusillade of laser fire and torpedoes as they hurtled over the treetops toward her. She adjusted her stance on the escape pod—feet apart, knees slightly bent—and raised her lightsaber.

"AHEEEEEEEEE!" a familiar voice screeched across the sky. Lula looked up just in time to see a winged shape blast down from the clouds and careen directly into the cluster of approaching Nihil ships amid a tangle of explosions.

"Vee-Eighteen?" Lula gasped. The enemy fire was already on her, though, and there was no time to stare. She slanted her lightsaber upward and swung away the first fusillade of laser fire, sending it directly into the approaching torpedo.

Ka-BLAAM! It exploded above her.

Up ahead, the newly modified V-18 had already smashed up two ships and was chasing down a third. The two Bonbraks sat on top, squeaking and cheering him on as they made small repairs and adjustments.

Five raiders were still speeding toward Lula, though.

It wasn't over yet.

"A living thing is very much like a machine," Master Kunpar once said when Ram complained about having to do anything besides his repair work. "The Force flows through organics, yes, and that is different, but we also have engines that keep us running, hm? We have central processing units, and when something is leaking, it slows us down, sometimes stops us entirely."

It had frustrated Ram at the time. He knew it was true in a way, but the problem wasn't all those moving parts and how they connected. The problem was organics—sentient ones, anyway—had opinions and judgments, and ways of doing things, and ways of *not* doing things, and opinions and judgments about those ways of doing and not doing things, and, and, and . . . It was all too much, really. And no theory or metaphor was going to change that.

But now . . . spine-covered branches sprang toward Ram and Zeen, who were both bleeding from various scratches as they blasted and slashed away. The control panel needed transmission vortices, and there was barely any sky to be seen beyond the attacking Drengir.

The Drengir were organic, though, and Master Kunpar said organics weren't so different from machines in certain ways. If Ram could fix or break mechanical things with the Force and if he could (more or less) mess with the minds of organics, he should be able to do at least something with these angry plant jerks.

"Cover me a sec. I'm going to try something," he said, and Zeen nodded, still cutting and hacking at each approaching branch.

Ram closed his eyes and reached out with the Force. Immediately, a thick, bristling wall of heaviness reared up to meet him. The Drengir's own Force use swamped the air. Whatever it was, Ram thought, it was something very far from the light.

He picked one squirming strand and felt its essential life force pulsing, the movement of nutrients through cells, the flow of the Force. It lurched and seethed in sudden bursts, but Ram finally got a lock on it.

Then he squeezed.

The Drengir's Force ability seemed to rush forward, partially blocking Ram's own, but he kept his hold, even as the rustling around them rose to a fever pitch.

"WHAT IS THIS, MEATS?" a Drengir demanded.

They were still calling him meat, but it was the first time they'd addressed him directly.

Ram opened his eyes. The attacks had stopped. Zeen glanced at him, bewildered.

"Why are you attacking us?" Ram said.

"*You* attacked *us*, meats!"

Ram had to suppress the wave of anger rising inside him. "*We* are just here to fix our communication tower," he said, "because we were attacked by the same raiders that brought you to this planet!"

There was a rustle and whisper as the Drengir seemed to consult with each other. "The Nihil?" one asked.

"Yes," Ram said. "They dropped you off last night, right? As seedpods."

"Well-informed meats."

"What did they promise you?"

"Promise?" The Drengir sounded aghast.

Ram wasn't fooled. "You didn't just allow yourselves to be planted on a faraway planet for fun. They promised you something in return for helping them out, didn't they?"

There was some more conferring. Zeen took a step closer to Ram, her eyes zeroing in on the shivering creatures around them. Ram had noticed it, too. Even though the attack had stopped, the Drengir still crept closer and closer in that chilling, slow plant crawl.

Explosions and laser fire had been erupting steadily in the sky around them. Ram could only hope it was Lula and the sanval laying waste to the Nihil.

"The raider meats promised if we took over this tower and held it off from anyone trying to fix it, we could have this whole planet full of supple pliant meats just for us."

Ram had to suppress the chill that slid through him.

CHAPTER TWENTY-ONE

"They told you the meats would be easy pickings, didn't they?"

"Mmmm, served right up on a platter and ready for devouring, yes," the Drengir agreed, and Ram noticed little shimmers of wetness on all the leaves—they were salivating.

"Live meats, they said?" Ram tried to make his voice sound skeptical.

"Drengir only eat meats that are alive. What is the point otherwise?"

"They lied to you," Zeen said, and Ram was glad she'd caught on to where all this was going.

The whole tower shook with the Drengir's incredulous roar. "WHAT?"

A rumble of engines grew suddenly louder, and Ram spotted a familiar flash of bright purple between the Drengir's branches and leaves. "Vee-Eighteen?"

"Master Ram Jomaram!" the droid called. Breebak and Tip yelped excitedly.

"What is this?" the Drengir said, opening up a wide breach to reveal a newly modified V-18 floating in the air. "This is not meat!"

"Vee-Eighteen," Ram said. "What . . . what did you guys do?" The droid had definitely made some adjustments in the short time they'd been separated. It looked like he'd somehow gotten his hands on a small craft and appropriated some of its parts, with the help of the Bonbraks. An impressive new auxiliary thruster stretched back beneath a sleek vectoring fin. And he had wings—bulky, retrofitted orange ones complete with external shields and a whole rack of missiles peeking out.

"Long story," the droid mumbled evasively. "Do you want me to blast away all these ugly weeds, though? We did add a flamethrower unit to my frontal core processor." Tip fiddled with a control panel, and a little burst of flame spouted out.

"Small furry meats with fire!" the Drengir hollered. Spine-covered branches swung out, poised to strike. "Must destroy!"

"Wait wait wait!" Ram yelled. "No fire! No fire! Hold on!"

"The weeds are talking," V-18 said. The Bonbraks only had rude, untranslatable comments to add.

"Everyone calm down!" Ram said. "Drengir, we're not

going to burn you down. Stay focused. The Nihil meats lied to you. That's what matters."

"Drengir hate liar meats most of all."

"Vee-Eighteen, did you happen to swipe a comms system off any of the starships you were stripping?"

"Why, sir! I reject the very—"

"*Bon-bala,*" Breebak and Tip both confirmed.

"Perfect!" Ram said. "Does it have transmission vortices?"

"Why, Master Ram," V-18 objected. "My newly enhanced class-A starship transmission vortices are directly wired to my vocalizer. If you take them out, I won't be able to speak!"

For a brief moment, everyone just stared at the droid.

"Wow," he said. "I see."

"We'll get you new ones as soon as we're out of this mess, Vee-Eighteen, I promise. Now get in here!"

*F*waZZshoooom! A laser blast hurtled past Lula, close enough to singe her sleeve and . . . She glanced down, then gasped. A small patch of skin on her arm had been burned clean off—there was just bright tissue there. The pain hadn't even reached her yet, only the utter terror of having been grazed. Shock.

She looked up just in time to see another series of shots blasting toward her. She sprinted up the wing of a *Grus*-class shuttle toward the cockpit. The part she'd been standing on erupted into flames, and the ship veered dangerously toward the ground. And then the pain hit, like someone was slapping her arm over and over with a spiny whip.

Lula skittered over the bulkhead, ducked beneath the dorsal wing, and then slid down to the far side and threw herself against the engine compartment to catch her breath.

The droid had taken out a good handful of Nihil ships before she'd even had a chance to catch up with him. She'd downed her fair share, too, so it made sense to send V-18 to check on Ram and Zeen. She figured she could handle the remaining half dozen attackers.

Badly burnt and tired to her core, she wasn't so sure anymore.

Her hands shook as she extended her saber and stood. The sky and treetops seemed to whirl around her. Had she pushed herself too far? It didn't matter. She couldn't stop. Ram and Zeen needed her help. Valo and the whole galaxy did, too. She shoved her saber directly into the narrow strip of metal connecting the dorsal wing to the hull of the shuttle. She felt it bristle and burn all the way through. Then she ran toward the tail end, dragging her saber along beside her. The wing shook and then began to tilt toward her. She used the Force to shove it the other direction and then threw herself forward just in time to let a new barrage of cannon fire shriek over her head. The shuttle rocked sideways, taking blast after blast—these raiders really had no aim whatsoever—and then tilted toward the ground.

Lula stood, ran even as the tilt steepened, then leapt through the air, grabbing a top rung of the tower ladder with one hand and slamming against it with her whole body.

For a few aching moments, she just hung there, panting. The burn on her arm pulsed shrilly through her.

She had to focus. Starships circled nearby; she could hear the ferocious growl of their engines, their weapons systems whirring and swiveling on their turrets.

And then, very suddenly, they were gone.

Which was worse, Lula realized, pulling herself onto the nearest platform.

All six Nihil ships had dipped lower, surrounding the tower exactly where Ram and Zeen were huddled amid angry, bristling Drengir.

Lula's diversion had failed.

"They've been attacking our city all morning," Ram insisted.

"Deceitful meats!" the Drengir growled. "But they haven't killed any Valo meats, right? Just buildings belonging to the meats for to make easier pickings. They promised us those meats! Alive meats!"

"Of course they killed your meats!" Zeen said.

Behind Ram, the Bonbraks fussed irritably with V-18 and the comms unit. He heard a few clicks and clanks amid their high-pitched banter but couldn't gather much from that. Anyway, they were out of time.

"See?" he said, pointing out beyond the vines and branches, where various Nihil ships had dipped low, weapons systems fully charged. They were zipping in circles around the tower—too fast for Ram to latch on to any one of them long enough to do damage. "There are your benefactors. About to light us all up."

"TRAITOR MEATS!" the Drengir yelled in a single raspy voice.

Ram lit his lightsaber. It all seemed so pointless, but they had to try. Zeen readied her blasters. And then something—no, some*one* landed in a crouch on the platform next to them. "Hey," Lula said, igniting her own saber. One of her sleeves was torn, revealing a nasty, shiny burn on her arm. "How's it going?"

"Fanfan paloooo!" a Bonbrak exclaimed.

"Almost there but out of time," Ram said.

The ships opened fire.

The first shot tore through a bunch of branches, sending woodchips and leaf flakes flying everywhere, and then slammed directly into Ram's saber.

Across the platform, Lula swished and swung, batting away blast after blast.

Ram deflected two more, and then a shot blew past him, zinging directly into V-18's wing with a crispy *thwunk*.

"Vee-Eighteen!" Ram and Lula yelled at the same time.

Tip chattered something at them and quickly got back to work. "He's okay," Ram translated. "Mostly."

See the whole for the whole, Ram reminded himself. *Each part for the role it plays.* Somewhere in his imagination, he was back in his garage, the most peaceful place he knew, with a dozen speeder parts hanging in the air around him, their inner workings a well-memorized map in his mind. There were only six Nihil ships. *Not for what you want it to be.* But he wasn't in his garage, and the ships wouldn't stay still long enough for him to do anything to them. And he plus Lula plus Zeen only made three, plus a droid and two Bonbraks. . . . *Not for what you fear it to be.* But maybe with a little help . . . There was only one way to make it work, Ram realized, but he didn't know if he'd be able to do it while deflecting cannon fire.

"Lula," he said, blocking two more shots and stepping backward. "Zeen."

"What do you need?" Zeen was ducking behind a

support beam, taking shots whenever she could through the Drengir's branches.

"I need you both to cover me, 'kay?"

They both nodded, ready.

"Drengir!" Ram yelled.

"Meat?"

"Meat speaks!"

"What says meat?"

Ram tried to add a commanding tone to his voice, one that sounded like he knew what he was doing. "I know you're mad! I need you to focus that anger. Specifically on the orange flier and single-pilot bomber, and those two Z-trawlers shooting at us. And the Cumberjumper and that, whatever that rusty thing is—can you handle those? Just keep them still!"

Ram swatted away another shot as the plant creatures conferred with each other. His arms were aching, and he felt like his mind was on fire.

"When?" came the grumbly reply.

"NOW!" Ram yelled.

Zeen holstered her blasters, took the lightsaber Ram

held out to her, and stood at the ready. Beside her, Lula batted away a couple of bursts.

The vines and leaves rustled, then quaked. Then, with a sudden wrenching and crashing, branches shot outward on all sides, blasting through windscreens and wrapping around landing gear and heating ducts.

All the Nihil ships around them shuddered, trapped in place.

Ram closed his eyes and reached out with the Force.

He would see the whole for the whole, each part for the role it played. He flinched as another shot slammed into the steel nearby him, sending cruel quakes through his bones. He would see the whole for the whole, each part for the role it played. He adjusted his stance and reached out again, harder this time, wider.

There! He felt each whirring machine around him, felt the Force move through him.

The whole for the whole, each part for the role it plays.

He reached into the orange flier and wreaked tiny havoc on its circuitry, engine valves, exhaust systems. He could feel the pieces click into place around him, remembered each one from his grease-stained handbooks. Wrecking things was so much easier than putting them back together!

The Cumberjumper started fizzling and smoking as soon as he used the Force to crunch its exhaust pipe shut. The flier was already spiraling toward the ground, the pilot jumping out with a shriek.

The bomber was more complicated, and as soon as he tapped into it, he could feel the craft start to shudder free of the Drengir's grasp. It wasn't moving yet, though! The landing gear was tucked away beneath huge metal plates, but wrecking those wouldn't help much. Just above them, Ram knew there should be an intricate circuit board that kept the main engines running, yep, and beside it the fuel tank—a fuel tank, Ram realized, calibrated to maintain a certain degree of pressure, since that class of bomber ran on zylium 12, which would solidify if not kept under the exact right atmospheric specifications!

That'd do it.

He reached with his mind toward the tank, then shoved outward with the Force. Immediately, the zylium 12 tightened into itself, and then the whole tank burst outward

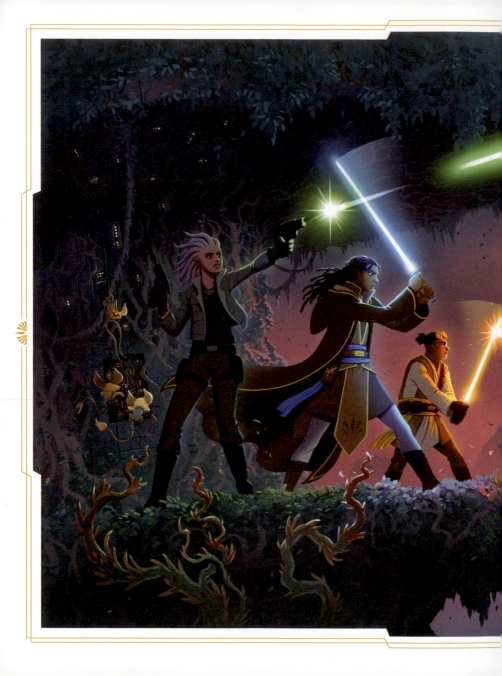

with a sharp bang, frying the circuit board instantly.

The bomber reared backward and then hurtled toward the trees.

The clunker was already wrenching free from the Drengir's viney grasp when Ram got to it. His eyes flew open to see the ship's front cannons exploding to life directly at him, and then . . . with a *fwooosh*, two light-sabers crossed in front of him—Lula's and his own. The laser barrage zinged away into the sky, and the two girls ran in opposite directions, each along a length of Drengir branch.

They moved like they were extensions of the same person—not a word exchanged. Lula leapt off one of the trawlers, which was too busy trying to free itself from the Drengir's death grip to even notice, and Zeen the other.

They met halfway across, in the air just above the clunker, and both dropped down, lightsabers extended. Within seconds, the ancient ship was reduced to a flaming wreck. Lula and Zeen leapt off together just as it began a steep plummet toward the ground.

"MEATS!" the Drengir roared. Explosions burst out

of one of the trawlers. It spun backward, firing in chaotic bursts, before a single vine wrapped around its turrets and sent it smashing into a tree.

"Whoa!" Ram yelled as Zeen and Lula landed on the platform in front of him.

One ship left.

The Drengir had left the second Z-trawler mostly intact, Lula noticed. Their vines were wrapped firmly around it, but they'd refrained from penetrating its windscreens or major parts. As a result, the ship was about to swing itself back into position to fire on them.

Lula had barely caught her breath, but there wasn't time. She dashed across a trembling bridge made of Drengir toward the trawler, careful to avoid those thorns. A side compartment slid open, and three Nihil scattered out onto the wing, blasters blazing.

Lula parried one shot and sent another zinging back into the ship, and then she was on them, lightsaber singing through the air in an unstoppable arc through the lead Nihil's blaster rifle.

They all stopped shooting, blinked at her, and leapt off the wing to the forest below.

Lula had to stop herself from running headlong into the belly of the ship, carried by all that momentum.

She allowed herself a moment to catch her breath, then glanced back as a tremendous crunching sound erupted behind her.

"THANKS, MEATS!" the Drengir yelled in a rickety cacophony of voices. Lula lunged to the side as an immense blast of wood and leaves rocketed past her into the ship. "We'll take this one, yes."

"But—" Lula started, but the Drengir had already shrunken themselves to fit their suddenly smaller quarters and were fumbling around for the door controls with twig tendrils.

"Planet no good."

"Comms now fixed."

"Reinforcement meats on the way."

"Deal broken."

"How will you—"

The side compartment door zipped shut, and Lula had to run and jump back to the tower as the ship banked into a sharp turn. She grasped one of the rungs, and then Ram and Zeen pulled her the rest of the way up. The Z-trawler lurched forward, slammed into a tree, and then veered hard into another before blasting skyward.

"Drengir can fly?" Ram gaped.

"Not very well, apparently," Zeen said as the two trees creaked and then collapsed.

CHAPTER TWENTY-FIVE

"**W**ell, that was—" Ram started to say, but he was interrupted by an urgent yelp from the Bonbraks.

"Fadooo kopa kopata!"

They'd hit a dead end on the comms panel repair. Ram whirled around, and the whole of it seemed to slide into place before his eyes in an instant: There was the link calibrator, the cord leading to the power renewer, the transmission vortices. . . . A little curl of smoke rose up from the inner chamber housing one of the secondary vector grills . . . which meant the vortices were overloading the system . . . which meant if he reduced its output load some, it should click everything into place. And he could do that by yanking one of the bright red wires from its base. "This should"—he pulled, and immediately the panel whirred to life with a series of blips—"do it! The comms are up!" Ram yelled.

Everyone let out a breath, then a cheer.

Suddenly, static filled the air.

Then voices. So many voices.

"Hello hello?"

"Can anyone hear me?"

"Come in! Sec Leader Seven! Come in!"

"Help!"

"We're under fire! Send—"

"Master Gios, is that you?"

The comms were up! And the whole city was realizing it at once, sending scattershot messages back and forth.

"We did it!" Lula yelled. "You all okay?"

Everyone nodded, blinking through their surprise. The Bonbraks jumped up and down on the comms box. Beside them, V-18 waddled in a circle, apparently all right.

"Valo Security Force. Assembled Jedi," an authoritative

voice came over the comms. "This is Stellan Gios. Please respond. Repeat—"

More voices filled the air, everyone checking in excitedly.

"Um, Padawan Ram Jomaram here," Ram said into the mix. "Sir."

CHAPTER TWENTY-SIX

They'd beaten the odds and survived both Nihil and Drengir, and helped salvage some kind of win amid all the terror. It would tip the balance, and Lula was sure once they got word out, Starlight would send reinforcements and they'd save Valo.

Lula heard Vernestra on the comms, calling out coordinates to something, and Master Sy. Even her old friend Master Torban Buck had shown up somehow—she heard him yelling about how he was on the way to save somebody, talking in the third person as always.

She got on the air herself once things had calmed down a little, let them know she and Zeen were okay.

Whatever happened next, the Republic, the Jedi Order, the galaxy itself would never be the same, and Valo had been the fulcrum on which the whole sea change had pivoted.

She'd been striving to find her own balance in the Force—it was a part of her journey to becoming a Jedi Knight that she'd come to accept amid all the chaos of the past few hours. But now she knew it wasn't just her—the whole galaxy teetered dangerously between order and chaos, peace and absolute war. It would find balance, though, Lula thought, and she would be a part of that balance. One way or another.

All that lay ahead, sure. But first, they had a city to help save.

"Let's go," Lula said, hopping on V-18 behind Ram and Zeen and then helping the Bonbraks into their side pouch. They zoomed off over the treetops.

TWENTY-SEVEN

The trees whizzed by beneath them, and up ahead, Ram could already tell the Jedi Vectors were ruling the skies. He watched as one swung past a small squadron of Nihil fighters. They gave chase, swarming after the Vector in a wide curve that placed them directly in the sights of about twelve other Republic ships, which blasted them from the sky in pieces.

Ram could barely believe they'd survived, let alone helped the Republic gain the upper hand. He'd always imagined himself living a quiet life on Valo, repairing ships and hanging out with his Bonbrak buddies and V-18 until he was a wizened Jedi like Master Kunpar. And that seemed all right to him. But in the span of barely a day, he'd watched the city he loved get torn apart; even more important, he'd done something about it. He'd made new friends, and suddenly the larger galaxy, with all its politics and machinations, seemed very close to home.

He'd seen the whole for the whole, and it meant there was no difference between little Lonisa City and the wider galaxy. They were all one, all connected, all part of a gigantic system—just like the floating speeder parts—and each had whole universes inside. They fit together and played their roles, and now he knew, more concretely than anything he'd ever known before, that he had his own role to play. And he would.

The radio chatter seemed to melt away as one commanding voice took over the air and started delivering instructions to the Jedi. Ram couldn't quite make out the words over the whipping wind, but it sounded like something important was about to happen.

"Lula," he said, turning back to his new friend, "when this is over, I want to join you. I want to see the galaxy and help the Republic." He was pretty sure Master Kunpar would be okay with that. He'd always told Ram that a Padawan should go out and explore the wider galaxy. Ram had just never paid him that much attention.

Lula smiled and nudged Zeen. "We were just talking about how we hoped you would!"

"You were?"

"Of course!" Zeen said. "And anyway, we need all the help we can get!"

Ram didn't know what to say. He turned to face front again, beaming on the inside, and then his mouth dropped open.

That was what the chatter had been about on the comms! Up ahead, the thick fog of the Nihil's war gas was suddenly dispersing, whooshed away as Jedi across the city used the Force to clear the skies of Lonisa City.

Ram threw his fist in the air and felt the galaxy widen around him as they zoomed toward home.

ABOUT THE
AUTHOR

Daniel José Older, a lead story archi-
tect for *Star Wars: The High Republic*, writes the
monthly comic series *The High Republic Adventures*, where you
can find out more about Lula, Zeen, and Ram. He is also
the *New York Times* best-selling author of the sci-fi adventure
Flood City; the upcoming young adult fantasy novel *Ballad
& Dagger*, book one of the Outlaw Saints series; the middle
grade historical fantasy series Dactyl Hill Squad; *The Book
of Lost Saints*; the Bone Street Rumba urban fantasy series;
Star Wars: Last Shot; and the award-winning young adult
series the Shadowshaper Cypher, which was named one of

the best fantasy books of all time by *Time* magazine and one of *Esquire*'s 80 Books Every Person Should Read. He has won the International Latino Book Award and has been nominated for the Kirkus Prize, the World Fantasy Award, the Andre Norton Award, the Locus, and the Mythopoeic Award. He cowrote the upcoming graphic novel *Death's Day*. You can find more info and read about his decade-long career as an NYC paramedic at danieljoseolder.net.

ABOUT THE ILLUSTRATOR

Petur Antonsson is a freelance illustrator for publishing and animation who lives in Reykjavik, Iceland. His full name is Pétur Atli Antonsson Crivello, and he was born and raised in Iceland by his Icelandic mother and French father. He graduated from the Academy of Art University in San Francisco in 2011 with a BFA in illustration. Petur worked in the gaming industry in San Francisco before moving back to Iceland, where he's currently doing freelance illustration work for various clients and companies around the world. He is represented by Shannon Associates.